To Don,

Bless

Pastor
12/13/13

I John 2:17

MW01243640

The Gospel According to Mary, Mother of Jesus

As presented in a letter written to her son, Joses

by
Donald W. Bartow

WHOLENESS PUBLICATIONS
CANTON • OHIO

Scripture taken from the King James Version of the Bible.

Wholeness Publications books may be ordered through booksellers, online or by contacting:

Wholeness Publications LLC
2221 Ninth Street, SW
P.O. Box 36057
Canton, Ohio 44735
www.wholenesspublications.com
(888) 799-6923

10 9 8 7 6 5 4 3 2 1

ISBN
978-1-893042-16-2 (hardcover)
978-1-893042-17-9 (e-book)
978-1-893042-18-6 (audio)
978-1-893042-19-3 (pdf)
978-1-893042-20-9 (large print)

Library of Congress Control Number: Pending

Printed in the United States of America.

Table of Contents

❧

Dedication

❧

I dedicate this book about the Holy Family to my family: my wife, Mary Elizabeth, who looked after the details of family living while I spent countless hours working on the book. Our daughter, Beckie, and son, Dennis, who gave of their insights and talents to help with it. Our five grandchildren: Allison, Dennis II, Brett, Nathan, and Aaron who have brought us great joy. And, our eight great grandchildren: Daryn, Gracie, Calvin, Ruby, Annabelle, Abigail, Elizabeth, and Beau, who have added much to our already abundant joys of a loving family.

Acknowledgements

❧❧

There are many who have been an influence as well as a tangible part of my writing *The Gospel According to Mary, Mother of Jesus.*

I am very appreciative of the many parishioners of the churches I have served, and how they have contributed to my walk with the Lord.

I certainly must thank John and Nancy Stevenson for their helpful suggestions and encouragement.

Victor Carsten, my friend of over fifty years, is worthy of very special thanks for his eagle eye and tender heart. These attributes have served him well as he helped his long time friend with this book.

I certainly cannot neglect extending a word of thanks for the ancient writers who have left us a biblical account of the life and ministry of our Lord and Savior, Jesus Christ.

Thanks to Christina Uduefe for her unique contributions of cultural aspects based upon knowledge gained through her extensive travel and missionary experiences in foreign lands.

My special thanks to Sandra Zirngibl, for her skillful editing of the manuscript.

I am grateful for all at the Total Living Center who have been an encouragement to me. Those who serve, as well as those who are served, are a daily inspiration and blessing to me.

In conclusion, I want to say that I appreciate all of the unnamed individuals who have offered suggestions and encouragement. I extend special thanks to those who read the manuscript and conveyed their helpful insights to me.

Although I have received an abundance of help from others, the bottom line is that I must, and do, assume full responsibility for any shortcomings of *The Gospel According to Mary, Mother of Jesus*.

Introduction

❧❧

The main reason I am writing *The Gospel According to Mary, Mother of Jesus* is to attempt to convey that ordinary individuals are used by God to bring His message of love to the world. Mary was a normal Jewish teenager. Neither she, nor any of those associated with her, were aliens from outer space. They were citizens of Planet Earth.

Brief Description

The Gospel According to Mary, Mother of Jesus is a very moving and personal account of the life and ministry of her special Son, Jesus. Creatively it presents the essence of the Gospel of faith, hope, and love. This is an entertaining and compelling read for the young, old, believer, or unbeliever.

It flows tenderly from the heart of the aged mother of Jesus. It is scripturally sound, culturally sensitive, and in modern language. Although spiritually powerful, there is still a very touching human quality throughout Mary's entire Gospel.

Reading the Bible

Many reading *The Gospel According to Mary, Mother of Jesus* will never have read the Bible. It is my prayer their reading my historical novel will inspire them to read at least the four Gospels. Maybe some will end up reading the entire Bible.

This novel will be read by some who have read the Bible often. I believe after doing so, they will look at scripture differently. They will be more prone to appreciate how those who knew Jesus, as well as those of the early church, may have thought and felt. It will help the average person to believe they are important in the sight of God, and with His help, can do extraordinary things.

In addition, I pray all who read this novel will have a greater appreciation of what Christians should believe, and how they can pursue a lifestyle of love for God and others.

Paraphrase

I present *The Gospel According to Mary, Mother of Jesus* as a paraphrase of an ancient letter dictated by Mary to Bocheru, her best friend's husband. It is not an effort to present a Gospel in the language such as found in the King James Version. It is written in the language of our day. It is not in classical English, but a novel comprised of common everyday expressions and language.

I write as I think an aged and devoted mother would write to her and Joseph's son, Joses, about her very special Son, Jesus. It is written as a personal letter might be written. Thus, for instance, events are not always in chronological order, but as they naturally come to Mary's mind. In addition, once in awhile she repeats herself.

Historical Novel

The Gospel According to Mary, Mother of Jesus is a historical novel. Is it all factually true? Of course not, it is a novel.

Is it at least partially true to the realities of daily living in the days of Mary? Yes it is. It is obvious I cannot prove that everything I have written actually happened. How can anyone know what Mary, Joseph, Jesus, and the many associated with his birth, ministry, and death said, felt, or believed? Even biblical scholars often do not agree on what actually happened in the life of Jesus. For instance, some accept the miracles, others do not. Some accept the body resurrection, while others do not.

Is my novel consistent with the Bible? Yes, it is. In the Biblical Index I list the scripture references for many of the biblical incidents I refer to in the book.

I have presented events as they may have happened, and how the participants may have spoken and felt concerning them. In spite of its acknowledged short-comings, this easy to read novel conveys many meaningful spiritual truths.

The intent of this novel is not to be absolutely culturally accurate, while at the same time being culturally sensitive. It is spiritually challenging as well as a very interesting and compelling read. It seeks, in a modern way, to convey ancient truths that will inspire and help individuals today to become more in love with Jesus.

Secularism is on the rampage in our country, and throughout the world. We definitely need an increased, and more specific, emphasis upon the spiritual. In my novel I may at times trample book format and culture, but I seek at all times to trumpet spiritual truths.

Chapter and Verses

This novel is written in chapter and verse form to have it appear more like scripture as we know it. Further, the verse numbering will help to quickly locate portions being discussed by friends, or by participants in a group who are using the book as a study guide. The verse numbers are in smaller type than the text. This enables you to read the book while hardly noticing the numbers.

Questions for Your Consideration

The Gospel According to Mary, Mother of Jesus is an excellent book for group study and discussion. It reads like a compelling novel, but teaches essential Christian truths as adequately as a text book. At the end of the book there are suggested questions for discussion concerning each chapter. They will be helpful for group discussion, or for ones private meditation. Hopefully they will stimulate you to raise more questions, and to seek the answers for them. The desired end is that you will be led to believe as never before in the Lord Jesus Christ as your Savior and Lord.

Biblical Index

The Biblical Index is an effort to help in your reading and study of the Bible. It lists the biblical references to many of the topics being considered in *The Gospel According to Mary, Mother of Jesus*. Even though it is a novel, I seek to be faithful to the Bible. The Biblical Index lists the chapter and verse in *The Gospel According to Mary, Mother of Jesus* where there are biblical details about the topic being considered. The Bible verse(s) dealing with the topic are then listed.

Bold Type Numbers

Throughout the novel, the number of the verse relating to a specific biblical reference is in bold type. These verses are the ones appearing in the Biblical Index with appropriate Bible reference verses. You will often find it helpful to read some of the verses prior to and after the ones listed in the Biblical Index.

Scripture Cross-References

The Scripture Cross-References with the content of *The Gospel According to Mary, Mother of Jesus* lists the book, chapter, and verse(s) pertaining to the many biblical topics and incidents Mary discusses in her letter to Joses. To the right of each Bible reference is the chapter and verse in Mary's letter where the scriptural topic or incident is considered. The Scripture Cross-References dramatically reveals how consistent Mary's letter is with the writers of the Old and New Testament.

Picture of Mary

The beautiful picture of Mary on the dustjacket of this book depicts her as a pensive and pondering mother struggling with the mysteries of the birth and ministry of Jesus as well as the cruelty of his death. Her Gospel deals principally with the years when Mary was a young woman. Keep in mind she was only a teenager when Gabriel appeared concerning her being chosen to be the mother of the Savior of the world. Yes, Mary was a young obedient handmaiden of the Lord and is a remarkable example of how an ordinary person can be used of God to accomplish an extremely extraordinary task.

This unique statue of Mary used in the photograph was created by an artist from the Netherlands in 1609 and is located inside the Great Saint Martin Church in Cologne, Germany. The photograph was taken by the author's son, Dennis W. Bartow, who resides in Bavaria.

The Ordinary Becomes Extraordinary

Read, enjoy, and may your own mind and heart be inspired to more fully appreciate how just ordinary individuals can be used by Almighty God to accomplish His purposes. It is not beyond the realm of possibility, that in the days ahead, you, as an ordinary individual, may experience an extraordinary personal and powerful spiritual encounter.

Chapter 1

❧

1 My dear son, Joses, I think you are right. I should share some of my experiences as the result of my being the mother of Jesus. I have so many fond and vivid memories of his life and his close friends. 2 Matthew, Mark, and Luke have written about him. A friend of mine has read to me all three of their efforts to tell his life story. But they leave out so much. 3 I realize a big part of the reason for this is that they only knew Jesus from the time he started his public ministry. So far, my big problem concerning writing a letter to you has been that I cannot read or write. Thus, I have never been able to write what is burning in my mind and heart about Jesus.

4 One day I was sharing with a neighbor lady, my best friend, how I would love to write you a letter of my memories of Jesus. With tearful eyes and a hurting heart, I told her that I was like other women. I could not read or write. So I couldn't do it. 5 A few moments later she responded with, "Mary, my husband, Bocheru, can help you. He is a very learned man. If you would tell your story to us, he could write it for you." 6 My heart leaped for joy at this possibility. I had her ask Bocheru if he would do this for me. He enthusiastically agreed. Now I can get a letter off to you.

7 There is no one who knows more about Jesus than I do. These dear friends come to see me every few days. I spend several hours telling them my story. 8 Bocheru writes down what I tell him. He is really good at this. I will be sending the letter to you in the not too distant future. I will try to keep it to a reasonable length for Bocheru's sake, as well as yours.

9 My telling about Jesus is from the viewpoint of being the one chosen by God to be his mother. I am the one who was more intimately related to him than anyone on earth. 10 None of the disciples knew Jesus until he started his public ministry. My parents, and others of my family, never even saw Jesus until he was over six years of age. 11 You see, after his birth, because of my health, we stayed in Bethlehem for about a year and a half. Then we had to flee to Egypt. We were there for over four years. Thus, it was several years after his birth that we returned to Nazareth.

12 None of the other disciples will be writing about him in the future. The news I have gotten from Israel is that all of his twelve disciples, except John, are dead. 13 How sad that Judas hung himself after betraying Jesus. What a tragedy. He was always different, but I never dreamed he would betray Jesus, or that he would ever take his own life. 14 I have gotten reports that Andrew, after being cruelly beaten seven times, was crucified in Achaia by being nailed to a cross in the form of an X. 15 Dear James, one of the very first of his disciples, was beheaded under orders of Herod Antipas in Palestine. 16 Phillip was so precious. He became known as the great soul winner. He was brutally beaten and crucified by the magistrates of Hierapolis. 17 They tell me Bartholomew was skinned alive and then crucified by a Roman governor in Armenia. 18 Thomas may have been a doubter at times, however, I can assure you

that he became a great and staunch believer. He was shot to death with arrows by the Brahmans in India. 19 It is believed Matthew was murdered at Naddabar in Ethiopia. He was the one I had the most doubts about when Jesus chose him to be part of the twelve. 20 But I must say the hated tax collector became a loving and fervent evangelist. He loved to hold dinners and invite his wealthy friends, as well as some of the poor and social outcasts. He would then tell them about Jesus.

21 I have heard that James, the son Alphaeus, was thrown from the pinnacle of the Temple at Jerusalem. 22 It is a strange twist of events that Thaddaeus was cruelly put to death by Magi of Persia. This really troubles me as it were Magi who came to worship Jesus at our home in Bethlehem. 23 Some say Simon the Canaanite was crucified. Others say he was cut asunder with a saw. Either way is a terrible way to die for being a just and holy man trying to help others.

24 I am not quite sure what to believe concerning Matthias. He was the one selected to take the place of Judas. I have heard that he was crucified. I have also heard he was stoned to death, and yet another rumor is that he was beheaded. However, whatever cruel way was used, he was killed for believing in and teaching about my precious son, Jesus.

25 I was devastated when I heard Peter had been crucified in Rome. How I loved that big friendly man. He was so full of life. Outspoken yes, but big-hearted almost to a fault. 26 They tell me he willingly laid down on the cross. They didn't have to force him to do so, as they did with others. The touching thing to me is they say he laid on the cross with his head down. 27 A soldier yelled at him to turn around with his head up. Peter responded, "Please, I am not worthy to be crucified as my master. Please, let me die

upside down." 28 Even the hardened soldiers could not deny this devout dying man's last request. They honored it, and crucified him with his head down.

29 Can you imagine how heavy my heart is, and how difficult my life has been? My son was killed. Now, eleven of his original chosen twelve are dead, plus Matthias who was chosen to take the place of Judas. Only John and I remain of those who were really close to Jesus. 30 I feel it is absolutely tragic so many good and holy young men have been killed, and at the hands of evil men. It just doesn't make sense to me.

31 With all that has happened, I must say I can better understand why Jesus instructed John to take care of me. He wanted to make sure someone looked after his beloved John. He is the only one of the twelve still living. Where would I be if I had gone to be with one of the other disciples? 32 As I have grown older it has dawned upon me I have not only been a help to John, but how precious it has been for me to have him care for me.

33 I now believe Jesus realized John had been the closest to him, and knew that he would be able to explain many things to me that I had never been able to understand. 34 John and I have spent countless hours talking about Jesus. We have discussed at depth what he taught, how he lived, and what he tried to impart to others. They have been sacred and informative hours. I never would have learned all of this from any other disciple. 35 And I repeat, I also believe Jesus wanted to make sure that John had someone to look after him. John was a young man, and Jesus evidently realized that by devoting my life to John, it would be a blessing to both of us.

36 I have urged John to write about his life with Jesus. He was closer to him than any of the other disciples. Further, after the Holy Spirit came, John had even greater

understanding of the teachings of Jesus. 37 He not only personally knows what Jesus taught and did, but he also understands the deeper meaning of many of these experiences. Jesus explained a lot of them to him as they often had long and very personal conversations. 38 It always seemed to me Jesus loved John more than any of the other disciples. Perhaps it was that he was so young or maybe it was because he more fully perceived the true spiritual meaning of the teaching and lifestyle of Jesus. 39 He insists he is not worthy to write about these sacred things. However, I am praying and believing that someday he will change his mind and share with the world his remembrances of the teachings of my son. 40 He just keeps saying, if a person were to write all that Jesus taught and did, the whole world couldn't contain the books. 41 I keep telling him there is a lot of truth to that, but at least he could put down some of the things that really stand out in his mind and heart. 42 I believe he will ultimately do it. Maybe, after he gets back from exile. He is now exiled on the Isle of Patmos, as the authorities want so desperately to silence him.

43 John is such a remarkable man. He has that amazing ability of talking one-on-one. Practically everyone he spends time with ultimately accepts Jesus as the Messiah. It is amazing. 44 He is so down to earth. He convincingly conveys how Jesus is the way, the truth, and the life. Also, miracles surround him as they surrounded Jesus.

45 As you know, we came here to Ephesus several years ago. John really felt the Holy Spirit was leading him to come here to tell the city about Jesus. He always wants to do what he feels the Spirit is leading him to do. I admire him so much for his faithfulness. 46 I pray the persecution in Israel will end. It was really a blow to me when they killed your brother James. I pray for God's protection of all

of you children. **47** We arrived in Ephesus shortly after a follower named Paul was here. He led so many to accept Jesus that the coppersmiths tried to get him killed. **48** He was putting their idol making business out of business. As John and I got the story, Paul appealed to Caesar and was sent to Rome. Some years later he was beheaded. **49** Now John arrived in Ephesus with his low key, but very appropriate approach. Many were having their faith rekindled, or were confessing Christ for the first time.

50 It was only a matter of time until John also became a threat to the greedy town merchants and to the jealous religious leaders. They decided to get rid of John in a way that would put fear in the heart of believers. Also, they wanted to put a stop to any who might be thinking of following the teachings of Jesus. **51** So they publicly tortured him. Then, they tried to kill him by putting him in a cauldron of boiling olive oil. I will never forget that day. **52** I really never thought they would do it. Then when I saw the pile of wood under a cauldron of oil, I felt my heart would burst. **53** I thought about how Jesus had been cruelly crucified. I about lost it. Then it flashed through my mind that all but one of his disciples had been martyred. Now the last one was about to be killed. **54** Deep in my spirit I felt I could not take any more. My legs were so weak I could hardly stand. My heart continued to ache. My hot tears practically burned my checks as they flowed so abundantly. I wanted to close my eyes to all of this horror, but I couldn't. I just had to see what I did not want to see. They paid no attention to my feelings. **55** The oil was bubbling, boiling hot, as they lowered John into it. There was no doubt he would be cooked alive. The last disciple of Jesus was being martyred. **56** It flashed through my mind: how horribly strange, that all of the close disciples of the one who taught the abundant life would soon be dead. **57** I could see John was saying something when they put him in the oil, but I couldn't make out his words. He told me later he was talking with Jesus and praising him.

58 All I know is that at the time, I felt the last of those close to me would now be gone. But here again in a very dark hour, a miracle took place. This has happened so often in my life. 59 John was not at all affected by this boiling oil! The wood burned to ashes. The oil cooled. John crawled out of that cauldron. 60 You should have seen the look on the faces of those who tried to kill him! They were absolutely astonished, and quaking in fear. 61 It was beyond me that he came out of a cauldron of boiling oil with perfect skin. I assure you it was much easier for me to now believe the three Hebrew young men really did survive the fiery furnace.

62 The common people saw John's deliverance as a miracle of God. The religious were not about to acknowledge a miracle had taken place right before their eyes. The leaders were so frightened they decided not to try another attempt to kill him, but to send him into exile. 63 Thus he is now on the Isle of Patmos. I am still in Ephesus being cared for by some relatives who have lived here for years. John may be isolated from other believers for a time, but the Lord will speak to him. 64 The political and religious leaders think they have silenced him. I think the world will still hear from him. I am not sure how, but God will provide a way. Mark my word! I am convinced he will end up doing some very important writing about Jesus. I truly believe that due to his knowledge and understanding of Jesus, he should, in writing, try to convey to others what Jesus taught and how he lived. He knew and understood him too well not to do this.

65 Oh, there are a few more things I would like to say about John being put in the boiling oil. He said that as they

started to put him in the cauldron, he saw the oil bubbling and thought it was the end. The troubling thought of what would happen to me was on his mind. 66 He went on to say as he was submerged into the oil it felt comfortably warm. Since he was not dying, he heard one of the men shout to a man near the cauldron to push his head under the oil. 67 Those close to the cauldron responded that they were not going to touch him. He said they seemed to fear for their own lives if they touched him. They finally ran out of wood and the fire went out. 68 None of us can explain how John survived. But we all saw it with our own eyes. Even these many years later, I cannot fathom why everyone that day was not convinced John was a devout man of God. Or that they were not convinced there was a powerful God whom John serves and who protects him. What will it take for the world to believe in Jesus? This is a question I often ponder.

Chapter 2

ঔ৵ৎ

1 The house John purchased after we arrived in Ephesus has served us well. One of the things I like about it is the crystal spring in the backyard. It never ceases to flow. It supplies all of our water needs. 2 Almost every time I go to get water, or someone brings water into the house, I think of Jesus. He said that he was the water of life. And strange as it may sound, he said the one who would drink of it would never thirst again. 3 What a unique way of imparting the fact that to believe in him as the Savior of the world would satisfy ones spirit completely and forever. What a precious truth, and to think it was my son who was able to teach it. This, among many other things concerning him, is still beyond my comprehension.

4 It has been many years since I became John's house-keeper. After the death of Jesus, the girls and I moved in with John to care for him. You boys continued to live in our home and to care for the carpenter shop. 5 I guess Jesus knew I would need something to occupy my mind and time, so he added John to my responsibilities. Of course, he knew John would take good care of me. He was always like a son to me. 6 John never married. He never really admitted it, but I knew he needed a woman to look after him and to help him. I was most willing to become his mother. He readily agreed to become my son. The girls later married

and had their own homes. 7 I have remained with John as his housekeeper these many years. We had no idea we would end up in Ephesus. When he felt led of the Spirit to come to minister at Ephesus, I naturally said I would go with him. 8 I felt Jesus knew what he was doing when he gave John to me and me to John. John definitely needed someone to care for him. I needed something to make my life more meaningful. My being his mother has worked out well for John. His being my son has brought a lot of precious joy to my life. 9 You might say, helping him has been what has kept me going all these years. And I am grateful that all of you children have been able to establish your own homes.

10 Joses, I am going to tell you something now that I have kept a secret from everyone, including the family, all these years. Your father and I, because of Jesus, were many years ago abundantly blessed financially. It happened when he was about eighteen months old. 11 Here are the details. When the Magi visited baby Jesus they gave him gifts. We have shared this fact with friends, right after it happened, and through the years. Years later we shared the visit of the Magi with you children and told you of their gifts to Jesus. We have not been reluctant to mention the Magi's gifts to Jesus were gold, frankincense, and myrrh. 12 However, all through these many years, we have never told anyone the true value of these gifts. After your father died, I talked to Jesus about the fact that we should tell you children of the riches. I reminded him our law and tradition is that the eldest son inherits the father's wealth. 14 As you very well know, our tradition and practice is that women never receive an inheritance. It always goes to a man.

15 Jesus really reacted negatively to our traditions concerning transfer of wealth. He said, "Mother, to whom were the gifts given?" I naturally replied, "They were given

to you." 16 His response was, "You are correct. They were given to me. They are mine, not yours, or Joseph's. How can you give wealth to the eldest son that is not yours in the first place? Further, have I thus far been willing to let you use some of this wealth as needed?" 17 "Yes, you have," I responded. Jesus said, "Well, Mother, there is one thing I want to make very clear to you at this time. Unreasonable traditions that preserve ridiculous ways should be broken. Men and women should not be kept in bondage because of them."

18 I was really getting nervous by what he was saying. This didn't seem to bother him as he shared more with me. He said, "Mother, don't you remember how the angel said to you that you would be blessed among women? 19 You need to realize this blessing was not only intended to be spiritual, but also material. I stress again, I know that putting you in charge of this wealth is contrary to tradition. 20 But I want you to know with certainty, it is what I feel should be done. And further, I want to tell you that before my earthly life is ended, I will have violated many traditions. 21 Believe me, I will be breaking a lot of them. This is one way I can help to really set people free. I won't need wealth. The Father will take care of all of my needs. So I have no problem saying to you that what is mine is now yours. Please, do not fret over my breaking a tradition." 22 With that, the conversation ended concerning the gifts the Magi gave him. As far as family and friends are concerned, the wealth received from the gifts were spent years ago. 23 There is no doubt I have certainly been materially blessed because of Jesus. Jesus definitely wanted me to keep and use the wealth as needed. 24 I am sure you can understand how I have thought a lot about what he did for me after your father died. Obviously it was different from the customary way things were done with wealth.

25 Even though I was glad to have the wealth, I was still bothered by being in charge of it. After all, I was a woman. This was not supposed to happen to a woman. I was really bothered by this blessing. Finally it dawned upon me. Jesus had only done what was his natural way of doing things. 26 He was different, and he often did things differently from what was traditional. Once I reached this conclusion, I realized more than ever that many things about Jesus were different. 27 His birth was sure different! His being conceived by the Holy Spirit was different from any pregnancy of the past, and surely from any since that time. There has been, and there will be, only one child born without an earthly father.

28 His walking on the water was different. It is difficult to believe it actually happened. But I believed Peter when he personally told me of his experience of taking a few steps on the water. 29 He said he deeply regrets he didn't keep believing and walking. However, when he saw those big waves, he felt they were going to overwhelm him. Peter really felt he was going to drown. 30 He never has been able to figure out how Jesus was able to save him from drowning, or how they both got into the boat. But what was most puzzling to him was that almost immediately, after he and Jesus got in the boat, they were at the shore. 31 Their large heavy boat was full of men and equipment. Somehow it went from being in the middle of the sea to instantly being at the shore. That was one thing he could never figure out or understand.

32 Jesus coming forth from the tomb was certainly different. His ascension back to the Father was different. I began to realize he did actually live and teach differently, and with an authority the religious leaders never possessed. The religious were really bothered by his methods and message. The common people loved them both.

33 However, even from the common person's viewpoint, one of the most reckless and ridiculous things he ever did was to touch a person who had leprosy. As you know, those with this dreaded disease are completely shunned. No one is to go near them, let alone touch them. Jesus not only touched the leper, he healed him. **34** I even heard that one day he spit on a person's eyes and they were healed. Another time he put mud on a person's eyes and told him to go wash in the pool of Siloam. When he did that he instantly received his sight.

35 Jesus also healed individuals on the Sabbath. This got him into trouble. It was especially true the time he healed an invalid on the Sabbath and told him to take up his mat and go home. **36** This infuriated the leaders. They were deeply disturbed because his methods were different from their law and their traditions. Especially since they taught that nothing should be carried on the Sabbath. They would rather a person remain ill and crippled than to be healed on what they felt was the wrong day and in the wrong way.

37 I must tell you that time and again, I heard from others that the common people really liked the way Jesus taught. They said he taught as one with authority, and not as the Scribes and the Pharisees. **38** I recall the time we discussed his instructing his chosen disciples. I asked how unlearned and ignorant men like he had called would ever be able to teach others. I was concerned about how he was going to advance his message and methods. His answer was much different than I ever dreamed. **39** He told me he would be sending a master teacher. This teacher would teach all who believed in him. My response was, "How can any one teacher teach all who need to be taught?" He said, "Mother, you don't understand. The teacher I am talking about will come to anyone who believes in me and in my Father's love. **40** Believers will not need things written on writing

tablets or a scroll. The master teacher will teach by imparting my truths on each believer's heart."

41 I personally witnessed the master teacher at work on
the day of Pentecost, and in my life, and the lives of other
believers since that day. 42 What I am attempting to say is
there were many things different about Jesus. Time has
clearly revealed he told the truth when he said he would
trample on a lot of traditions. He certainly did. He really,
really did.

Chapter 3

❧❦

1 It has been seventy-one years since the angel Gabriel visited me. It doesn't seem possible it has been so long ago since Jesus was born. I remember how it took place as if it were yesterday. 2 You know, Joses, I am now eighty-six years old. Your father has been gone these many years and I certainly don't have many years left. 3 I find constant comfort in what Jesus told me when I remarked to him one day about the fact that he was hardly ever home. I was sad I seldom saw him after he started his public ministry. 4 He said to me, "Mother, don't you worry. There will be a time when we will never be separated. You will be with me forever. 5 Someday I will leave this earth, but I will come again. I will come for you and all others who believe in me. We will then be together forever." 6 At that time, I couldn't comprehend what he meant. Even so, his words were a comfort to me.

7 Joses, I am so grateful you have come to realize in recent years that you never really knew Jesus, even though he was your half-brother and you grew up together. You thought he was crazy. Surely you remember how you and your brothers ridiculed him. 8 One day you boys nagged at me so much about what people were saying about Jesus and our family, I sent you out to tell Jesus we wanted him to come home. 9 You and your brothers were really upset with

his response to your request. You returned and told me he refused to come back with you. In fact, you said he gave you a odd answer. 10 He said to you that anyone who believes in him, and does his will, is his brother, sister, father, and mother. This convinced you children more than ever that he really was crazy. 11 It always pained me to see you boys so often, and so cruelly, put down your brother. I knew that the angel had told me he was to be the Savior of the world, but I could never convince you children this was the case. You thought of him as being crazy and not as being a Savior. 12 But such is all behind us. He was killed. Your brother James has been killed. And Joses, sometimes I fear for your life, and the lives of your brothers and sisters.

13 I can't understand it. Jesus did so much good, yet some want to erase all of his wonderful and helpful teachings off the face of the earth. Their hatred is so strong that many of his followers are constantly persecuted and some even killed. 14 In addition to all the problems I have mentioned, there are some other very important aspects I want to share with you. I want to set the record straight to the best of my ability. 15 There are many false things that have been said about Jesus. A number of them exist to this day, and some are even gaining in intensity. 16 It is hard to believe how some people cling to rumors as if they were true. They seem to far prefer rumors and lies to the truth. I am sure you have heard some of these things. 17 The religious leaders have accused him of being a bastard, implying he was born out of wedlock. Yes, it is true that Jesus is your half-brother. But that is because he was implanted in me by the Holy Spirit prior to my marriage to Joseph. 18 I can't emphasize it enough that I did not become pregnant by some young Jewish man or by a Roman soldier. I can emphatically state that Jesus is not illegitimate. In some ways he is the most legitimate son

ever born. His Father is God.

19 Others called him a drunkard, even a blasphemer. There is more. Some to this day insist he is an imposter. 20 There are those who actually claim he is the son of the devil himself. They even accused him of doing his miracles through the power of the devil. Can you believe this? 21 How can anyone believe the devil would be doing what is really good for individuals, such as making them walk, see, or hear?

22 Oh, it gets even more bizarre! It is being taught by some so-called religious people that Jesus was not really human. He only seemed to exist. They are teaching that when he walked along the seashore there were no footprints in the sand. 23 They go so far as to say that he really did not die on the cross. It just seemed that he did. How? Why, such teaching? I just can't figure it out. 24 Joses, I was there. I know. He bled, he suffered, he died. Oh, how well I know he died. In a sense, I died with him that day. I didn't think I could go on even with John's help.

25 It gets even more ridiculous. The teaching of no earthly father is now being applied to me. Believe it or not, some are actually teaching that I had no earthly father. These people are teaching that I was implanted in my mother's womb by the Holy Spirit. 26 Your grandmother and I talked a long time about this one. She told me, "Child, I can assure you that your father was there the night you were conceived. Believe me, he was there. 27 It is easy for us to pinpoint the night you were conceived. The next day your father left on a business trip that lasted over six months. I definitely was not pregnant prior to his leaving. 28 Several weeks after he left, I realized I was pregnant. I certainly had not been with any other man, and no angel showed up with any out-of-this-world announcement. Yes, you can believe me. My husband is your father."

29 As if that is not bad enough, the teaching has gotten around that Jesus was my only child. This rumor started even before your father died. We sometimes actually laughed about it. 30 True, it was over six years after Jesus was born that James arrived. James was my first child with Joseph as the father. But after James, you, John and Simon came along. 31 Our last two children were girls. I assure you they were the apple of your father's eye. He was so proud of them. The truth is Joseph was proud of all of his children. 32 Your sister, Salome, would often go with me to hear Jesus teach when he was in our area. Your younger sister stayed with some of my relatives when the two of us would be gone for several hours or a few days.

33 Joseph was so kind to me. He certainly tried to make our home God-honoring and a happy place for all of us. I still remember him saying after your youngest sister was born, "Mary, now we have seven. Seven is the perfect number." 34 Shortly after she was born, your father died. I can assure you that Joseph is the father of you six children. 35 I recall the times your father would say, "Mary, I am a blessed man. As I got older I began to think I would never marry. And of course, it was just too much for me to even dream I would have children. Now, I am not only happily married, but I have Jesus and my other six children. Yes, I am blessed."

36 I suggest you ask anyone about me who lived in Nazareth when we were there. They will assure you I went around pregnant several times. All six of you children were born within a span of thirteen years. Do believe me. I birthed all six of you, and Joseph is your father.

37 Jesus was my firstborn child, but I definitely had six more. Some have even gone so far as to say all of you kids were cousins of Jesus. 38 If they would have been at the synagogue the Sabbath Jesus taught, they would have been

aware of the fact that all the town folk knew you were his brothers and sisters. 39 It was one of the rare times he was home after beginning his public ministry. He was asked to speak at the synagogue. This he was very willing to do. 40 He earnestly endeavored to teach them not so much to seek to please God, but to really believe God. He related some of the great things that could happen if you truly believed. 41 He mentioned a number of miraculous healings which had taken place as he laid hands on individuals. This infuriated the religious leaders. The common people seemed to accept it, but the pious religious people were not willing to be open to Jesus' concept of spiritual power. 42 They reacted as if Jesus was just one of us. They even said, "Are not his brothers and sisters living right here in Nazareth?" They wouldn't accept him or his teaching. And he couldn't do many healings there because of their unbelief. However, he did lay hands on a few and they were healed.

43 Many at Nazareth may not have believed in what Jesus was doing. However, there was no doubt all knew I had been pregnant many times since coming to Nazareth. Their problem was how our ordinary family could have a son with the power Jesus talked about in the synagogue. 44 I can't stress enough that his being a member of our ordinary family, and yet claiming amazing spiritual power, was what led to their trying to kill him. 45 Urged on by the religious leaders after the service, a mob tried to take him out to the top of the hill to push him over and then stone him to death. 46 I don't know how it happened, but somehow he simply disappeared from the crowd. That really caused confusion. No one could figure out where he had gone and how he disappeared with no one seeing him go.

47 It remained the main topic of conversation in Nazareth for weeks. But never was it questioned by any

Nazareth resident as to whether or not I gave birth to other children after Jesus.

48 I must also mention that Luke believed I was the mother of other children. His account of the birth of Jesus reveals that I laid my firstborn son in a manger. This certainly leaves the impression that he knew and believed I had other children. **49** Joseph was very kind and patient after we were married. However, it wasn't until several weeks after Jesus was born that your father and I began to live as husband and wife. Truly you children are living proof of this. **50** Joses, I want to assure you that you are not a cousin of Jesus. You are his half-brother, and you have three brothers and two sisters. Please believe me.

51 But now I want to discuss another silly rumor about Joseph having children before we married. I hope I can finally debunk it once and for all. Please consider these facts. **52** If Joseph were a widower dutifully caring for six children prior to our being married, why did he treat them so indifferently after we were married? Let me explain what I am getting at. **53** Do you think for a moment if I were the caring step-mother of his six children he would have let me go to Bethlehem with him to register for taxation and leave them at home? **54** Or that I would even want to go and leave them with relatives or friends? Further, can you imagine what an experience it would have been if I were the step-mother of six children, and we took all of them with us to register for taxation? **55** Wouldn't it have been a full stable? And I can readily think of some antics you boys would have done. Joses, you probably would have tried to ride the donkey, and James would be teasing that old goat to the point he would have butted one of you. **56** I shudder to think what it would have been like with me having such a hard time birthing Jesus, and having six kids standing around gawking and crying.

57 Here is another important aspect to consider. Joseph and I spent over eighteen months in Bethlehem after Jesus was born. Your father was an honorable man. Do you think if he had six kids before our marriage, he would have burdened one of his relatives or friends with taking care of them for a year and a half?

58 It gets even more unrealistic when you really stop to think about it. Remember, we fled Bethlehem and went to Egypt. We were there for over four years. Jesus was six years old when we returned to Israel. When we left Egypt our intention was to return to Bethlehem in Judea and to buy a home there. 59 Now, think about this: If Joseph had six kids we had left with others in Nazareth, would we be planning to continue to live in Judea? It doesn't make sense, does it?

60 This rumor of my not having other children really bothers me. Now I must say, common sense tells anyone that Joseph and I had children together. We ended up in Nazareth because of Joseph being warned in a dream that Archelaus would kill Jesus if we returned to Bethlehem. We absolutely, positively, did not return to Nazareth because there were six children who needed their father and their step-mother. 61 We lived in Nazareth before James, the first child of Joseph, was born. I want to assure you once again that Jesus was brought into being by the Holy Spirit. 62 All of you children are the offspring of Joseph. Indeed, I am an ordinary Jewish mother, grandmother, and now great-grandmother. 63 I want to respond one more time to the rumor that Joseph had relatives rear you. If this were true, why would people at the synagogue associate you so closely with Jesus? 64 Yes, I was chosen by God as a young woman to bear his Son, conceived by the Holy Spirit. I also was privileged to birth four boys and two girls with Joseph as their father.

Chapter 4

❧❧

1 Joses, I want you to know more details concerning some of the many incidents surrounding the birth of Jesus. I was puzzled at the time, and have pondered many things in my heart after he was born. I am even more puzzled today and spend a lot of time thinking about the many things which took place at the time of his birth. 2 I can't forget the past even though I try to keep pressing into the future. I am sure you can understand why I have pondered many things in my heart over the long years. 3 As a very young Jewish girl, my mother taught me that someday a very special King of Israel would be born to a young Jewish virgin. For hundreds of years, thousands of young Jewish girls dreamed of being the chosen one. I admit I too had that dream. But I knew it was only a dream and would never come to pass. 4 Then it happened to me. An angel appeared before me and announced my being chosen to be the mother of the deliverer of Israel. The angel even told me to name him Jesus. 5 I truly only saw myself as a humble handmaiden of the Lord. Just think about it. My parents were devout, but very poor. They were not honored in the community. They were not special in any way. Yet, there appears an angel to their ordinary daughter saying I was blessed among all women. 6 You cannot possibly appreciate how my heart jumped with joy. My mind raced with visions

of golden days for Israel. 7 Strange as it may sound to you, when the angel told me the Holy Spirit would come upon me and I would become a mother, I never doubted him. 8 At the moment it just seemed the normal way it should happen. One sure thing, it never crossed my mind I would have so many heartaches to endure in the immediate days and following years. 9 Even though it was so far-fetched, I could readily and heartily accept it. I, an insignificant nobody, would soon be a true somebody as the mother of the deliverer of Israel. 10 The angel departed. I never felt afraid when he was with me, but after he departed I began to tremble. I became so weak I had to lie down for a while. I had a hard time comprehending I was going to have a child. And that I was going to have a very, very special child. 11 The problems relating to my being pregnant, even though I was not married, began to close in upon me. How was I going to explain this to my parents, my friends, and yes, especially to Joseph? Would he accuse me of adultery and have me stoned to death? 12 It was then a terrible fear of the future almost consumed me. Believe me, those were difficult days for me. Looking back, all those worries ended up minor compared to the hardships and agony I have had to bear because of Jesus. 13 He was such a blessed and special child. But oh, he brought special and almost unbearable worry and heartache to me. I must say I have learned a lot. 14 One of the most important truths I have learned is when you are told, even by an angel, that you will be blessed by the Lord, it doesn't mean everything is always going to be great. It doesn't guarantee the rest of your life will be free of troubles and sorrows. 15 Yes, when the angel, Gabriel, told me I was blessed among women, I couldn't believe my ears. My thinking then was, what a happy life I am going to have. 16 The old saying, 'she lived happily ever after', did not happen to me. Nothing could have been further from the truth. From the very beginning of the angel's message to me, I began to face obstacles. I don't mean just little nuisances, but real gigantic obstacles. 17 For instance, I was so thrilled that I was going to have a baby I failed to realize how hard it would be for a very young un-married teen-ager to be pregnant. 18 After coming down from the thrill of the angel's visit, I began to try to plan for my future. One of the first things that crossed my mind was how am I going to tell my parents I am going to become pregnant? Or do I wait until I become pregnant and then tell them? 19 I decided to wait until I was sure I was with child. But I found it was still a real problem. 20 They knew Joseph and I were engaged. How was I to explain to them I was with child, but we had never been together? I knew their immediate response would be to blame Joseph. 21 Then if I defended his innocence, they would really be dis-tressed thinking I had played the harlot. Of course, I was very worried as to what Joseph would do. How was I going to explain this miracle to him? 22 I knew my being with child was a miracle of God. He would probably perceive it as an act of inexcusable adultery. In fact, he might feel it was an unforgiveable sin! He would perhaps have me stoned to death. I broke out in cold sweat at that thought. 23 You know, Joses, a woman committing adultery is to be stoned to death. How could I ever convince him I had not done such a horrible thing? I can't begin to tell you how dreadful those days were for me. 24 No wonder my parents commented about my acting so strange. I am sure my anxiety about something was very evident to them. However, they had no idea what it was.

25 Shortly after I was certain I was with child, I told my parents. They reacted with shocked disbelief. They demanded to know why, and how, I could do such a terrible thing to them. 26 My father became furious and said he

would kill the man who did this to me. He naturally thought it was Joseph. He felt this older unmarried man had taken advantage of a young woman. 27 He practically shouted at me, "Mary, he will have you stoned to death. Don't you understand how serious this is? Don't you understand what your pregnancy will mean to your mother and me? We won't have a daughter much longer. Oh God, have mercy on our family." 28 They did finally calm down a bit. But believe me, they never really calmed down completely. It was then I told them the details surrounding the angel's visit. 29 My mother's response was, "Mary, you have never lied to us before. Why are you doing so now?" I insisted I was not lying or making up a story. What I told them was all true! 30 Eventually, they at least left the impression they half believed me. However, they were still very doubtful I was being truthful. 31 My father became distant. My mother almost went into a state of depression. Their constant worry was what will the relatives and neighbors think? And of course, what will Joseph do? 32 I had always been a model child and now I am a pregnant young woman claiming to still be a virgin. From their viewpoint, it couldn't get any more ridiculous than this, or any more frightening.

33 To me, facing Joseph was the biggest problem. It was evident he suspected something was wrong with me. He would say, "Mary, you are not your old self. What is wrong? What is the matter?" 34 I would respond with, "There is nothing the matter. I just haven't been resting well lately," or some other excuse. I didn't lie to him, but I certainly couldn't get up the courage to tell him I was pregnant. 35 Time naturally revealed I was pregnant. No longer could I hide the fact I was carrying a child. My pregnancy was evident to anyone looking at me. I finally told him. It was then Joseph became very blunt with me. 36 He expressed shock that I would be unfaithful to him. I

then told him the whole story. But he would have nothing
to do with it. 37 He felt it was just my attempt to shield the
guilty party, whom he felt was some young Jewish man, or
even one of the Roman soldiers. I begged him to believe
me, but to no avail. 38 I felt at any moment he would tell me
he was going to expose and accuse me. I knew our law that
a woman who is engaged and gets involved with another
man is committing adultery. I further knew this could mean
death by stoning. I was trembling on the inside. I was
practically numb with fear. 39 Then, after what seemed like
almost ages, he finally looked at me. His eyes were filled
with tears as he began to hesitantly speak. He said, "Mary, I
can't marry you. However, I will divorce you privately. I
could never bear to have you stoned to death. 40 You are too
precious to me, and too lovely a young lady for me to have
you stoned to death. I will lessen your pain as much as I
can. My big problem is how will I get rid of my pain? Yes,
rid of my aching pain of losing you? Mary, I truly do love
you." He then abruptly left.

41 Some days after I confessed to him, he stopped to see
me. He told me he had talked to the priest. The priest naturally told him it is impossible for a woman to be pregnant
without a man being involved. No one, and he said the
priest emphasized, no one, has ever been born in any other
way. The priest told him the honorable thing for him to do,
being an engaged man, was to have me stoned to death.
42 You can imagine how frightened this left me. I then
really tried to convince him my situation was different. It
was evident he was far from being convinced. He left me
with the absolute decision that he was not going to have
anything to do with me, or my child. He would reject me.
He would not marry me. He would never see me again. It
was all over!

43 I was heartbroken and cried out to the God of our fathers. He heard and honored my prayer in a very strange way. It was some days later, Joseph showed up at our house and asked my mother if he could talk with me. 44 When mother told me he was present and wanted to talk, I tearfully but defiantly told her I didn't want to see him now or ever. She agreed with me and told me she would tell him to leave, and never to come to our home again. 45 I heard her telling him in no uncertain terms I was too wounded to have him bring more grief to me, and he should leave immediately. I heard the door close and knew he was gone. 46 My heart was breaking, but I simply had to accept his decision to not marry me and that I could be stoned. To my surprise a few minutes later my mother was back saying, "Mary, you really ought to talk with Joseph." I couldn't believe my ears. 47 I said, "Mother, why do you pressure me. He is gone. Let him go. Can't you understand how I feel? Joseph thinks I am lying to him. He definitely believes I have been with some man. 48 Oh I know he claims to be an upright, honorable man and very religious. I know he does a lot of religious things to try and make sure he pleases God. But mother can't you see, I just want him to believe God. 49 I know the angel appeared to me. I know what he said is true, because I am now with child." She continued with, "I know all of this Mary, but it is very important you talk with Joseph." 50 She just kept begging and insisting. Finally, I relented and said I would meet with him for a few minutes, but that was all. I told mother I didn't hate him, but I sure didn't want to be around him.

51 Joses, you must understand mother didn't tell me until later that evening why she changed her mind and begged me to see Joseph even though I had defiantly refused to do so. She told me he did leave as she asked him to do. For some reason, she followed him out the door.

52 She said he had gone several steps when he slowly turned and came back to her. He then told her of a dream he had and now he wanted to marry me. That is why she came back and pleaded with me to at least talk with him. 53 She did not want to be the one to tell me the good news. She definitely wanted me to hear it from him, not her. But I want to get back to what turned out to be the wonderful part. 54 Finally, I reluctantly yielded to her request and met with Joseph. It was obvious when I came into the room where Joseph was waiting that I was not in a very good mood. I couldn't help myself. I was very cold toward him. 55 He asked my mother if we could talk privately. I was glad my father wasn't home, because he never would have let us meet privately. Mother didn't seem to be bothered by his request. I half-heartedly agreed to our meeting alone. 56 After my mother left, there was a period of very awkward moments of silence. Finally Joseph spoke to me. Haltingly he softly spoke his first words. They were, "Mary, please forgive me. I have wronged you and have been rebellious toward our God." 57 All I could say was, "Oh Joseph, Joseph," and I began to cry. He came close to me and took my hand in his and said, "Mary, last night I had a dream. In my dream an angel of the Lord appeared and told me not to fear to take you as my wife."58 I could hardly believe my ears. I honestly believe my heart almost stopped. This was the tender Joseph I had known and still loved. 59 I was definitely getting over my coolness and warming up to him. He was encouraged by my non-verbal response of warmth and told me, "The angel assured me you had been with no man. He told me it was true that the Holy Spirit had come upon you and, in spite of your virginity, had planted a child in your womb." 60 By this time, I was almost overwhelmed with joy and peace. The next few moments were about the most precious I have ever experi-

enced. It was then he said words I felt I would never hear. 61 He said, "Mary, please forgive me for not believing you and for being so mean to you. I want to marry you. Mary, I will marry you regardless of what relatives and neighbors may say about you. I believe you. 62 But even more than that, I believe God. I believe the angel which appeared to me in my dream was sent by God, and told the truth. I believe an angel was sent to you and that his message is true. I also believe the advice of the priest is wrong. Regardless of what he thinks or says, I know I should not have you stoned to death. 63 I should love you and your soon-to-be-born special son. Yes, I want to marry you and to care for your God-given son as if I were his father." 64 By this time I was most willing to listen to anything he wanted to say, and to spend as much time with him as possible. He went on to tell me something which really touched my heart even more. 65 He said he had already told his parents he was going to break off his engagement to me. He wanted them to know we would not be getting married. 66 But before coming to see me, he told them of his dream, and that the angel had convinced him to change his mind. 67 He told me his aged father said, "Joseph, do you realize what a blessed man you are? The woman you are to marry has been chosen to bear the child who will teach us as never before that God is with us." 68 He asked his father what he was talking about and how he knew this to be true. His father replied, "Joseph, many years ago the great prophet, Isaiah, foretold the coming of a very special child. 69 Isaiah wrote, 'Therefore the Lord himself shall give you a sign; Behold a virgin shall conceive, and bear a son, and shall call his name Immanuel.' 70 Don't you get it? This is that child. You are to love his mother, and to carefully and prayerfully help her rear her miracle child." 71 My mother had told me a young Jewish girl would be chosen to bear a special child. But she never told me this truth was proclaimed by a prophet of old. I took for granted it was a story as part of our tradition. But I sure appreciated Joseph sharing the prophecy with me. 72 I now had many reasons to be overjoyed. Joseph believed me. It was further confirmed I had been chosen of God to give birth to Israel's special son. Joseph was really happy. He was not going to have to live his life as a single man. At long last, he would be married. 73 In addition, he was willing to love and to care for this extraordinary one as if he were a child fathered by him. We were both really happy. 74 In these precious moments, he said to me. "Mary, maybe someday we can have children of our own." I blushed at this, and said, "Oh, Joseph, don't embarrass me. But maybe we will. We shall see." 75 Oh how happy I was that I had finally agreed with mother's request to at least talk with Joseph for a few minutes. 76 I now knew more deeply than ever I truly loved him and he loved me. But even more important, I now believed God loved both of us abundantly, and that Joseph and I would have a great life together.

Chapter 5

꙳ஜ꙳

1 We talked on for a long time. You can well imagine how relieved I was. Truly a heavy weight was lifted off of me. I was free. I was happy, oh, so happy. It was at this time Joseph offered the suggestion I should get out of Nazareth for awhile. 2 This sounded like a good idea to me. But where would I go? Mother agreed with Joseph and suggested I go see my relative, Elizabeth, who lived in Jerusalem. 3 I was so thrilled Joseph had returned, it didn't immediately hit me what a good idea it was I visit Elizabeth. I was, in a sense, walking on a cloud of joy. I knew my parents were thrilled Joseph was going to marry me. Their little girl would not be stoned to death. 4 To me, the most important thing was Joseph believe me and believe God. What more did I need? A few days later I departed for Jerusalem. I left Nazareth knowing I was blessed and all would work out well in the future. 5 I felt it was only a matter of time until everyone would believe me. I now know how foolish my thoughts were that from that time forward I would enjoy a pleasant life. It has been anything but a life of bliss. Believe me!

6 I had heard Elizabeth, even though beyond ordinary childbearing age, was pregnant. The story was her husband had been visited by an angel and was told Elizabeth would conceive, and they would have a son. 7 I was really anxious

to talk with her. I was especially anxious to hear about the angel's visit. I got a strange greeting from Elizabeth when I entered their home. 8 The first thing she said after cordially greeting me was, "Mary, when you came in, my baby leaped with joy in my womb. I feel it was a touch of God. With what Zacharias and I have gone through the last few months, I needed that touch. 9. For some reason, I now feel more relaxed and confident that things are going to work out alright for us and our son. Thank you so much for coming to see me."

10 We spent some time talking about our pregnancies. I related to her about the angel visiting me, and how the Holy Spirit had come upon me, and that I was with child through Him. 11 She said she had heard it rumored I was expecting, but she sure wasn't aware of the miracle aspects of it. She felt the same as others that I had gotten involved with Joseph or some other man. 12The last she had heard was Joseph was not going to marry me. I assured her I had been with no man, and that my child was truly from God. Further, that Joseph was going to marry me. 13 She asked me to fill her in on all the rest of the details. This I most willingly did. She then said, "I really can't tell you much of what happened to Zacharias, since he is not able to talk. I hope someday to hear the details of his visit by the angel. 14 He has written me notes about an angel and that we would have a son. It must be true because I am pregnant. I must say it has been difficult being around Zacharias with him being unable to talk. It has been really awkward and often very embarrassing for him and for me." 15 Elizabeth and I did a lot of talking about many things. It wasn't until after Jesus was born and we were staying with them for a few days, Elizabeth was able to tell me the details of their miracle child.

16 A few days after Jesus was born, we went to spend some time with Zacharias and Elizabeth. A day after we arrived and both of the babies were sleeping, Elizabeth said, "Now, Mary, I must tell you the rest of the story. 17 Those months when Zacharias could not speak were terrible. He would get so frustrated. We were one happy couple when his voice was restored. 18 After Zacharias got his voice back, he was eager to tell me the details of the angel's visit. You must realize we both had accepted the fact we would be childless. Then there was this special day he was caring for his duties at the Temple as the honored priest serving in the 'holy of holies'. 19 He had finished his duties, which ordinarily takes only about thirty minutes. He was about to come out and speak to the waiting crowd when an angel appeared to him. He was really startled to have a heavenly visitor. We don't know of any priest who has had an angel visit him. 20 Zacharias naturally was frightened, but at the same time felt very honored. The angel told him I would conceive and we would have a son. 21 Zacharias told me he laughed out loud when the angel told him I would bear a son. But there was no doubt the angel felt he had a message of truth to deliver. 22 The angel got real specific and told Zacharias we should name our son, John." I responded with, "Isn't it interesting the angel told you what you should name your child? And the angel visiting me told me what to name my child." 23 Elizabeth said, "Zacharias continued to doubt the truth of the angel's message. Then the angel told him that as a sign of the coming of our son being from God, Zacharias would not be able to speak until after the baby was born. 24 Yes, and you of all people, should understand why Zacharias had such a difficult time believing the angel's message. 25 Everyone knows I am beyond childbearing years. Yet, from an angel he gets this message I would have a son. You must under-

stand, we concluded this was not a convenient time for an angel's visit in our old age or even while Zacharias was ministering before the Lord. 26 A large number of people were waiting for Zacharias to come out to give them a fresh word from the Lord. But now, while talking with you, it occurred to me there is no perfect time for an angel's visit, is there?" "No, Elizabeth, I don't think there ever is," was my response.

27 She continued, "It gets complicated, Mary. As you know, the tradition is when the priest exits the 'holy of holies' he is to have a word from the Lord for the people. There are always a large number of people present to hear this fresh word from the Lord. 28 Zacharias said when he came out he was excited because a larger crowd than usual was there waiting for him. He sensed they were uneasy and he could understand why. They were bothered by his taking so long to come out to speak to them. 29 He was definitely in the 'holy of holies' much longer than a priest would ordinarily be. He said he must have been in the holy place for nearly an hour. He is not sure just how long it was. 30 It wasn't the angel that delayed him. It didn't take long for the angel to deliver his message, and he did not stay long. He vanished immediately after his message was delivered. 32 Zacharias said he couldn't help himself. He was so stunned he couldn't leave. He fell to his knees in prayer. It was several minutes before he could regain his composure and go out to speak to the people. 33 He found out later the other priests were also getting really worried about his taking so long, but they couldn't check on him. The law is unless the ministering priest dies in the 'holy of holies', or has a crippling attack of some kind, no other priest can enter.

34 "Mary, do you realize how traumatic this was for him? It is a great honor to be the priest selected to enter the

'holy of holies.' An important aspect of this is when you come out of the 'holy of holies' you have a special word from the Lord for the people. 35 With a visit from an angel and the news we would have a son, he had a very special word from the Lord. But Zacharias was not able to speak it. The crowd literally gasped as he opened his mouth, but nothing came out. They were amazed. Zacharias was stunned. 36 Again and again he tried to speak, but he absolutely had no voice. Disappointment set in for the crowd. After a few minutes, one by one they began to leave. Zacharias was almost frantic. He was really humiliated. 37 Sadly he is still looked down upon by the other priests because of this experience. He has never fully regained his stature among his fellow priests. There is no doubt his being unable to speak is by far the most embarrassing thing which ever happened to him. It still haunts him. 38 He found out later the other priests were also getting very worried about his taking so long to do his ministry. However, they couldn't go in and check on him. 39 As I mentioned earlier, our law is unless the ministering priest dies in the 'holy of holies' or has a physically crippling attack of some kind, no other priest can enter during this sacred ministry time.

40 "Now our little son, John, is living proof I did become pregnant. Zacharias and I praised the Lord for the angel's message. However, we were very troubled he could not talk." 41 It was obvious they both had been greatly troubled concerning Zacharias's affliction, while at the same time thrilled about having a son. She went on to fill me in on the details of John's birth, and how his father got his voice back. 42 They had interpreted the angel's message that Zacharias would be able to speak immediately after their son was born. This did not happen. They were really discouraged. They were beginning to believe Zacharias

would spend the rest of his life unable to talk. 43 Then her face brightened and she went on to say, "The eighth day we had our baby boy circumcised and gave him his name. Since Zacharias couldn't speak, I told them his name was to be John. The relatives reacted at this, as no one in the family had ever had this name. 44 I said, ask Zacharias what his name should be. This they did. He indicated he wanted a writing tablet. Honoring his request, I handed one to him. He wrote, 'His name shall be John.' 45 Then the miracle happened. At that very moment, his tongue was loosed and he began to speak fluently. The words of the angel had come to pass. We had just misinterpreted when it would be." 46 I then asked her what this experience has meant to Zacharias and how it has affected them. She said, "Oh my, it really touched Zacharias. He now says he never realized how involved he had become seeking to serve God, and how far he was from believing God. 47 He also now realizes the priesthood, to a large extent, has become a number of men furthering tradition more than individuals seeking to believe and serve God, and to lead the people to do the same. 48 To him, most of what they teach is as sounding brass or tinkling cymbals. It is his feeling Israel needs someone to rise up and call our nation to true repentance. He has no idea who that might be, but now practically every day he prays for this to happen."

49 I couldn't get Elizabeth's comments out of my mind. Many years later it came to me the priests did, to a large extent, teach the proper ways of God, but they sure didn't live them. Jesus certainly realized this fact. 50 I recall the time Salome and I heard him speak very strongly against the religious ones. He pronounced woe on them for their hypocritical and long prayers. 51 I vividly recall he told them they were like whitewashed tombs. He said such graves are pretty on the outside, but on the inside they are

full of dead men's bones. There was no doubt he felt they put on a good front, but on the inside were full of hypocrisy and evil. 52 What still perplexes me is the priests were not persecuted or killed for the wrong they taught and believed. John and Jesus taught vital and true faith and they also lived it. It still seems a tragedy to me both of them ended up being killed. It just doesn't make sense to me.

53 Elizabeth and Zacharias died before John started to preach. Sadly, Joses, they never lived to know their John was the one so mightily used by God. Yes, strange but true, their only son was the answer to the sincere prayer of Zacharias for someone to call Israel to true repentance. 54 I often wish they would have known John baptized Jesus and announced to the world Jesus was the long awaited Messiah. I must confess, when I visited Elizabeth and John, I had no idea of the important role John would play in the beginning of the public ministry of Jesus. 55 Looking back on our days with Zacharias and Elizabeth, who would have ever dreamed those two little babies peacefully sleeping near to one another would be used of God to change the world? Joseph and I sure didn't, and neither did Zacharias and Elizabeth, nor anyone else. Only God!

Chapter 6

ॐॐ

1 Even after these many years, when I think about the happenings which took place when Jesus was born, I am still puzzled and amazed. I have pondered the events surrounding his birth for hours on end. 2 I was possessed with the idea that the one who was to save his nation should be widely known from the moment he was born. I interpreted the angel's message to me as such. I wanted to make sure he was born in the right place. And that his birth would be known by the right people. The right place would be Jerusalem, and with the full knowledge of the religious community. 3 This led to some manipulation of Joseph on my part, but I meant it all for good. It also included an edict by the Romans concerning taxation. They sent out a decree in which all Israel should be taxed and everyone was to register for taxation in his own city. 4 Bethlehem was really Joseph's city, not Nazareth. He was of the lineage of David. Well, I didn't want Jesus born in that little town. I schemed a way, or so I thought, for him to be born in Jerusalem. 5 I can understand why Matthew, Mark, and Luke fail to mention many details surrounding the birth of Jesus. They did not even know Joseph or me at that time. They had no personal contact with the days of his birth, childhood, teen years, or the early years of his manhood. Therefore, they naturally just included major highlights about his birth.

6 Obviously, I was there through all of those years and I can tell you like it was. Joseph had to go to Bethlehem to register for taxation since he was of the house and family of David. You must understand this Roman ruling applied only to Joseph. I was not required to go. 7 In fact, he did not want me to go. He feared for me and our soon to be born child. By this time, he was referring to Jesus as our child, even though he knew he was not the father. 8 We knew it could not be much longer until Jesus would be born. Joseph felt I should stay in Nazareth to be near my mother when the child arrived. He was hoping he would be back in time, however he did not want to take any chances of it happening while we were traveling. 9 I reacted strongly to being left behind. I pointed out how I could ride the donkey, and that I would be doubly careful not to overdo it, as far as travel and caring of details, while on the journey. I stressed how he could take care of them. 10 I made my plea even stronger by saying I did not want to be separated from him the many days it would take for the journey. I said we could be back within two weeks at the most. I never realized it would be several years before we would be able to return.

11 Joseph sure didn't agree with my logic, but he yielded to my plea. He always did what I asked him to do. Maybe this wasn't right, but I liked it and he was willing. So what was I to do, but become a spoiled wife? 12 He really was a kind man, and I have missed him so much since he died over forty years ago. The journey was uneventful, yet not as easy for me as I had tried to convince myself and Joseph it would be. 13 It was late afternoon the day we got near to Jerusalem. Joseph wanted to stay there for the night with Elizabeth and see baby John. Then we would go on to Bethlehem early the next day. 14 It was I who insisted we press on to Bethlehem. He tried to tell me there would probably be no place to stay. The town would

be overflowing with visitors coming for the required taxation registration. We didn't have any relatives or friends in the area with whom we could stay. 15 Here again, contrary to his wisdom, we journeyed on. It was dark when we entered the little town. Joseph immediately sought a room at the inn. I couldn't wait to get off the donkey, get something to eat, and to relax in a room. 16 Lo, and behold, the innkeeper wouldn't even give Joseph the time of day. He said the inn was more than full. Every room was taken, and some were sharing their room with total strangers. 17 Joseph pleaded with him, explaining I was heavy with child and could give birth at any time. This seemed to alarm the nervous and almost exhausted innkeeper even more. Then he really wanted to get rid of us. 18 He rudely almost shouted at us, "Be gone! Don't you understand? There is no room in the inn!" We hadn't gone far until he loudly said, "You can spend the night in the stable if you want. At least you will be warm in there with the animals. It isn't fancy, but you will be out of the weather and it may even rain tonight." 19 I really got upset. In fact, I almost lost it with anger. I don't know how Joseph was able to so calmly handle my rage. He simply said, "Mary, please! Don't forget you were the one who insisted on coming with me. I tried to warn you of the difficulties and how hard it would be." 20 He emphasized, "And further, you are the one that insisted we bypass Jerusalem and get to Bethlehem today, even though we both knew it would be late when we arrived. 21 I am sorry we are ending up in a cave that is being used as a stable. But please don't be angry with me. Frankly, I am grateful we will at least have some shelter for you. 22 After all, a lot of families around Bethlehem live in caves. It serves as their home, and often at night their animals are right in there with them."

23 I insisted I was not going to sleep in some dirty cave.

Joseph tried to reason with me. He said, "Mary, when I was a boy, I often stayed with relatives who lived just outside of Bethlehem. They lived in a cave. I have often slept in a cave. It is at least inside away from any rain and the chilling wind." 24 I finally, out of desperation, yielded to his reasoning. We ended up at the stable. We discovered it was one of the largest stables in the area. It was used by those staying at the inn to keep their animals. 25 The innkeeper was correct about one thing. It was warm in there. He failed to mention it was also dirty, smelly, dusty, and crowded. We ate some bread we had in our pouch. Joseph prepared a place for me on the hay and a spot for him nearby. 26 It was close to the manger that I noticed had been hewn out of the stone. It was only a few feet from the nearest animal, a rather frisky and mean looking goat. Surprisingly, it only took a few minutes for me to fall asleep.

27 In the wee hours of the morning, I awakened with piercing pains which became more and more frequent. I was beginning to break out in a cold sweat from the pain, as well as from the fear of what might happen to me and my child. I screamed for Joseph. He sprang to his feet and began to care for me. 28 There was no doubt the child was about to be born. It was then I panicked. That which I feared had come upon us. Jesus, the promised Savior of the world, would be born in a place shunned and unnoticed by the world. 29 Now, how was the world ever going to hear about him? There were animals, but no people to behold the new born babe. 30 This added to the already many problems of giving birth in a stable. Further, it was not an easy birth. My screaming disturbed the animals. They became restless. 31 Joseph was so nervous. He was not sure what to do. Finally, the child was in his hands. Believe it or not, the baby's first cry helped sooth my shattered nerves. It also eased the pain and agony I had just gone through.

Chapter 7

༂ঞৎ

1 What were we to do? I had not brought items for an occasion like this. After holding the baby close to me for awhile, I took some cloth I had, and wrapped him in it. Joseph laid him in the manger. It wasn't long until he was sleeping. 2 I couldn't believe he was sleeping so peacefully. But I sure was not sleeping. Now I was not only angry at myself, I was beginning to get angry at the angel, and yes, even at God. The one who was to save his people is born in a stable. How ridiculous is that? 3 I must confess I began to doubt what I knew I heard the angel say about Jesus being the chosen one of Israel. How could a deliverer of a nation be born in a stable and anyone know about him? 4 Joseph couldn't get to sleep either, and we spent a long time discussing what we would do tomorrow and in the immediate days ahead. 5 It was certain that this long, hard journey and stressful birth had taken its toll on me. I was so weak I could hardly lift my hand to take Joseph's as he reached out to comfort me. I just kept looking at the little one, the Savior of his people. What a joke! 6 I couldn't help but wonder, who will ever know? How will the world ever learn of this miracle? Jesus continued to sleep. Joseph and I had finally dozed off. Some of the animals were already beginning to stir. The sun was just beginning to come up, when excitement hit our cave. 7 We couldn't believe our

ears when someone loudly shouted at the mouth of the cave, "Is there a baby in there?" Our hearts almost stopped with fear. Who would be asking such a question? Would they bring harm to newborn Jesus? 8 Sleepily Joseph responded, "Yes, yes, there is a baby in here." Then the man asked a strange question, "Is he lying in a manger?" Joseph replied that he was and asked, "Why are you asking such a question?" 9 The man didn't take the time to answer the question. He immediately rushed into the cave. We were able, in the light of the early dawn, to discern he was a shepherd. 10 He was followed by five or six other shepherds. The animals scattered as they came dashing in, but the shepherds paid no attention to them. They just kept stammering, "This is the one! This is the one! It is as the angel said. This baby in the manger has to be the one." 11 Almost at the same time, Joseph and I said, "What are you talking about? And what do you mean 'this is the one'? Who is he?" 12 Then they asked, "Are you his parents?" We thought that was a silly question, since we were the only humans in there. Certainly one of those cows was not his mother. We almost laughed at that question. 13 Then the one blurted out, "Do you know this baby is Israel's Savior?" "What?" We almost shouted! "Yes," they said. "The angel told us we would find him lying in a manger. We have checked out many caves, and were about to give up when you said there was a baby in here." 14 Joseph's startled response was, "An angel, what do you mean an angel told you something?" The shepherd said, "We were watching our sheep, as we do every night. Lo, and behold, an angel appeared in the sky. 15 This angel said, 'Do not be afraid, for behold, I bring you good news of great joy which will be for all the people; for today in the city of David there has been born for you a Savior, who is Christ the Lord. This will be a sign for you. You will find the baby lying in a manger.' 16 Then suddenly the sky was filled with angels. There were thousands of them. Their voices were beautiful beyond words as they sang in unison, 'Glory to God in the highest, and on earth peace among men with whom He is pleased.' 17 The angel and the multitude of angels were gone as quickly as they had come. We immediately decided to check out the angel's message. Our big problem was, he didn't tell us which cave. 18 Since they left, we have searched many caves for the child. We were about to give up, but now we are so happy we did not quit looking. Do you parents have any idea how blessed you are?" 19 Joseph answered that we could assure them we really didn't know. It was too overwhelming for us to fully understand what had taken place, and what would take place in the near and distant future. 20 We told them we really were not sure what the future held for us. We just wanted to be servants of the Most High God. Then in my heart I began to wonder. Could it really be God's will for Jesus to be born in a stable? Maybe God is in control after all. If the angels know about it, maybe the world will learn about Jesus, in spite of where he was born.

21 The shepherds sure felt God was in it all. They were so excited that, even though they were poor humble shepherds, the angel of the Lord had spoken to them. In addition, thousands of angels had appeared and sang for them. 22 They said they were going to go to Jerusalem and tell the high priest what had happened to them. They felt he should know, and that he would be thrilled with the message of the angels. 23 It was a few years later we heard that when they went to see the high priest, he wouldn't even take time to greet them, let alone listen to their story. They must have been a heartbroken bunch of men. God bless them. 24 After they left, I felt I should share with Joseph the reason I really wanted to come with him.

Through my tears, I told him I wanted to make sure Jesus would be born in Jerusalem. This way the religious people would know it. 25 Because of their position and influence, they could help spread the good news about the special one being born. This was the reason I had pressed him to travel on to Bethlehem instead of staying in Jerusalem for the night. 26 You see, my plan was that we would take care of the tax business in Bethlehem. Then we would go to Jerusalem to see baby John and visit with Elizabeth and Zacharias. They would be glad to see us and we could stay as long as we desired. 27 I had it all planned out in my mind that we would stay until Jesus was born. I knew it couldn't possibly be more than a few days. But I never thought his birth would be the night we spent in Bethlehem.

28 So once again, I experienced some hard moments. Looking back on them, I now realize the hand of the Lord was in it all. Life is indeed a mystery to me. Blessings and cursings seem to be companions. One good thing was some of the travelers departed the inn the next day, and we got a room there for five days.

Chapter 8

ॐ

1 We then went to Jerusalem and lived with John and Elizabeth for several days. When he was eight days old we had our baby circumcised and gave him the name of Jesus, as the angel told me to do. When my days of purification had ended, we took Jesus to the Temple to present him to the Lord. Since at this time we were very poor, we offered the sacrifice of two young pigeons. 2 I felt this would be the time when the leaders of the religious community would acknowledge him as Israel's deliverer. It was a great disappointment to me that they did not even mention that a special child of God was being dedicated to the Lord.

3 There was an old man there by the name of Simeon. He got excited. He told us the Lord had revealed to him he would not die until he had seen the favored one of Israel. He said Jesus was the one and that he would be a light to the Gentiles and a blessing to Israel. 4 Anna, a widow of many years, was also very kind. She was an elderly lady who spent many hours in prayer at the Temple practically every day. She tried to tell everyone about this special baby. They listened, but it was obvious they were not impressed. 5 So much for my feeling that being a friend of Zacharias would be the needed contact with the religious community. We discovered he was looked upon with suspicion, because of claiming to have been visited by an angel. 6 Even the

miracle of the birth of John had not convinced the other priests that an angel had spoken to Zacharias. They seemed to have a hard time believing in angels. It is so difficult for people to believe the spiritual. 7 They can readily accept and agree with tradition, but it is almost impossible for them to believe God really does appear to just ordinary people in extraordinary ways, such as with angels.

8 It was obvious, even after we had been with Elizabeth for about a week, I was not getting any stronger. The emotional impact on me because of the place of the birth of Jesus, plus the physical impact on my body, left me practically housebound. 9 Luke, in his account of the life of Jesus, imparts the impression we went back to Nazareth immediately after his circumcision and dedication. This is not really accurate. 10 There was no way I could have endured a journey back to Nazareth at that time. We stayed with Zacharias and Elizabeth for several days. Joseph searched for a job in Bethlehem. He found one and worked several days to earn money for a deposit on a rented house. 11 We were very poor. Most of what little we had when we left Nazareth was spent on the room at the inn. The house we rented was a very small one, but met our needs for the moment. We felt we would soon be returning to Nazareth, and so could put up with the very small house for a short period. 12 We were so grateful for the kindness of Zacharias and Elizabeth. Also, we just loved baby John. We intended to be in Bethlehem for only a few weeks at the most. Our intent was to stay until I got strong enough to make the journey home. 13 We never dreamed it would take me so long to regain my health. The weeks turned into months, and before we knew it, we had been there for over a year. 14 Joseph had made some nice furniture for us in his spare time. Although far from the nice home we had in Nazareth, it still was a comfortable little house. And it was sure a lot

better than the cave. 15 I was getting more homesick by the day. The better I felt, the more homesick I became. I knew mother and father were anxious to see their first grandchild, and, of course, were very worried about my health. 16 Jesus was a healthy and happy child. He walked before he was a year old. We were very proud of him.

17 As we, and many before us have learned, if you have received a special touch or calling from God, life is never dull for long. We were planning to leave for Nazareth in about two weeks when a strange thing occurred. 18 It was just before we went to bed when I noticed our one window seemed to light up. Then it was as if the light beamed through the window and shone on little Jesus who was asleep on his mat. 19 I called for Joseph who was in the other room. When he came to see, he too was surprised, almost afraid. What in the world was going on? We sure didn't know what was happening. Was this an omen of something important? 20 We went outside to look. Sure enough, there was a strange star in the sky. It was one we had never seen before. And it was so bright. We thought we were imagining things, but it really did look like it was shining on our house. It took us a long time to get to sleep. We could not get this strange happening out of our minds. Was it an omen of some kind? 21 The next morning, Joseph said he had not slept well and was not going to work until after lunch. He seldom missed any work, and so I knew he really needed this time to rest some more. 22 It turned out to be so right that he had stayed home, because at mid-morning there was a loud knock at our door. Joseph answered it, and talked with someone for several minutes. 23 I finally said, "Well, why don't you invite him in?" He did. And to my surprise a few moments later seven of the most elegantly dressed men I had ever seen were crowded into our small room. While they were coming in, I glanced

outside to see if there were more, because I could hear talking coming from the street. I was shocked. 24 The street was crowded with several more Magi, their servants, and armed guards. In addition, there were dozens of curious local folk. I thought, "And to think they are at our house." 25 After they left, Joseph and I talked about the large number of Magi and all the people they had with them. We could not understand why there were so many of them. Including the local people, it was certainly a large crowd drawn to our humble home. But when we finally opened the gifts they gave Jesus, we realized traveling with that much wealth you would need a lot of people for protection. 26 Also, those rich Magi were not going to do any cooking. And they were not going to put up the tents and prepare their own sleeping mats every night. They would never roll up the mats, care for the tents, or care for their animals for each day's journey. And they had been traveling for several weeks. So they brought a large number of servants to do this. 27 Further, this large company of people, with the special highly armed guards, would keep the ever present robbers from stealing their expensive clothes, jewels, tents, and gifts they had for little Jesus.

28 Now, I must get back to the ones who came into our house. Our room was small and their presence made quite a roomful. We were astounded when all seven of them fell on their knees when little Jesus came in from the other room. We couldn't understand what they were saying, but it was obvious they were worshipping him. 29 A few minutes later, one of them crawled forward on his knees to Jesus and presented him a gift. A second one did the same thing. Then a third one, carrying a somewhat heavier gift, crawled forward and laid it at the feet of Jesus. 30 We had no idea at the time what these gifts were. One thing we did know. They were sure beautifully and elegantly wrapped in

brilliant colored cloth. To me, they looked like gifts fit for a King. 31 One of the things which touched me was Jesus stood so still during all of this. It was as if he knew this was what he should do. I can't explain why, but I must admit my mind dashed down through the years. I saw him as a handsome young man being crowned King of the Jews. I was standing near him as the proud mother of the King. He was receiving all kinds of precious gifts from rulers throughout the world. 32 I was brought back to reality, when Joseph said to the one who spoke Hebrew, "What is going on here?" The man replied, "We have traveled far to find the King of the Jews and to worship him. The Lord has shown us Jesus is this person. Thus, we wish to worship him and give him gifts." 33 We were left speechless. I thought maybe my fantasizing about Jesus being a King was going to come to pass. I said, "But how do you know he is the King of the Jews?" 34 Their response was, "Oh, we know for sure he is. There has been a prophecy in our land for hundreds of years that someday a King of the Jews would be born. The world would know this because a special star would appear. 35 This special star appeared. We followed it until we arrived in Jerusalem. At the moment that didn't bother us, as we felt the King of the Jews had probably been born in Jerusalem. 36 Where else would such a famous one be born? But the star ceased to shine. We asked several where the one born King of the Jews was living. No one knew. They couldn't even grasp what we were asking about."

Chapter 9

ॐ

1 They continued with their story. "Somehow news got to King Herod about the King of the Jews being born. He invited us to his palace and asked us a lot of questions. He was especially interested when the child was born. We haven't yet figured out why he was so interested in his age. 2 We told him it was about eighteen months ago when we saw the star in the western sky. We presumed this was when the child was born." Joseph and I were startled and looked at each other, because we knew that was the age of Jesus. 3 Their amazing story continued. "Herod then asked us where he was born." They went on to say they could not tell him where he was born, because the star ceased to appear after they got to Jerusalem. 4 Herod then called in religious leaders and asked them if they knew where a King of the Jews would be born? They said a prophet named Micah had foretold his being born in the little town of Bethlehem. 5 You can imagine how shocked Joseph and I were to hear this. That is exactly where he was born, even though I had fervently sought to have it take place in Jerusalem. Joseph then asked, "But how did you know where our house was?" 6 The one who answered our many questions said they had arrived in Bethlehem late yesterday afternoon. They first asked some people on the street where the castle was. He said they only laughed at them. 7 That

response surprised them. The local people said there is sure no castle in this little town. Then they asked, "Well then, where was he born, the King of the Jews?" The town folk laughed again and said, "King, there sure is no king here. And even if there were, he would not be alive very long. Herod would see to that." 8 "But how then did you find our house, that is what I want to know?" Joseph asked. One of them related how the night before, after most had already gone to bed, he happened to go outside for a few minutes. He came back in all excited. He got them all up to go out to see the star which had reappeared. 9 They soon followed it and discovered it was shining on our house. They then knew they had found the place. It was evident they couldn't understand how it could possibly be the place. It sure wasn't a castle. In fact, it wasn't even a fancy house. It certainly did not look fit for a king.

10 They went on to say they could hardly wait to find out if a child were living here. I remember one saying, "We didn't want to bother you at night, or too early in the morning. So we have come at mid-morning, although it has been hard to keep from coming sooner." 11 Then Joseph told them about the strange light the night before, and how it seemed to shine upon Jesus as he was sleeping on his mat. These were exciting moments for them and for us.

12 They then continued to talk about King Herod. They said, "He was very cordial toward us. However, he didn't seem to be too friendly with the religious leaders. 13 After the religious leaders had revealed where the child would be born, Herod rather abruptly thanked them for their time. It was obvious he wanted them to leave immediately. 14 They left without showing any interest in our story about the King of the Jews being born. This seemed strange to us, as we felt they should be the ones really interested in this child. Herod seemed genuinely and deeply interested. He

then proceeded to ask us a number of questions." They went on to say, "He seemed genuinely interested in knowing about this new king. 15 He wished us Godspeed. He asked that once we found the baby king, we come back immediately and tell him where he was living. He said he was a very religious man and wanted to also come worship him. So we presume King Herod will be visiting you in a few days. 16 We must be honest and say that, although it appeared he really wanted to know and to honor the young king, at the same time there was something sinister in the way he spoke. 17 We shall be back in Jerusalem the day after tomorrow. We want to rest here in quiet Bethlehem today before beginning the long journey home. 18 Herod said we could spend a night as his guests, and thus be further refreshed to begin our long journey home. He said he would instruct his servants to give us a lot of supplies for the journey home." 19 One of the other Magi spoke up and said, "After we left Herod, we discussed how interested he was in the new born king, and how disinterested the religious leaders were. 20 In fact, they seemed to us to act as if they didn't believe our story. We really felt Herod believed it, and he sincerely wanted to see the child. 21 Yes, we really believe you can count on him, or his representatives, coming to see you within a few days. Just think, the ruler will visit your humble home, and worship your child. What an honor for you and your child. 22 We will make certain to let him know where you live. And we are looking forward to being his guests for a night."

Chapter 10

১Our visitors left happy they had found the one they were convinced was the King of the Jews. Joseph and I had our doubts about this King business. However, there was no doubt in their minds but that they had worshipped the King of the Jews. We sat in our humble home puzzled as to what was really going to happen next. I thought, the world is learning of Jesus even though he was born in a stable, in the little town of Bethlehem. God is doing it. It is a miracle. ২ If an angel told me of his birth, and if an angel told this to the shepherds, and if a multitude of angels sang for shepherds and if Magi were informed by a special star, then surely God would get the word out to the world in some way. I knew not how, but I was beginning to believe the world would hear of him. ৩ About an hour after they left, Joseph opened the gifts they had given Jesus. We were shocked. We discovered the heavy gift was several pounds of gold. Yes, it was pure gold. The other two gifts were expensive frankincense and myrrh. We were literally stunned. ৪ Even though Joseph had never been around such riches, he estimated their value to easily be thousands of dollars. We were no longer poor peasants, but rich parents of one born to be King of the Jews. ৫ I recall Joseph saying, "Mary, I don't know for certain if Jesus will end up King of the Jews. One thing I now know for sure is the gifts the

Magi presented to him are fit for a King." It was at that time I became firmly convinced my son was truly going to become the King of the Jews. This conclusion definitely remained with me through the years. 6 We found out later the gifts were much more valuable than Joseph had estimated. Is it any wonder we had trouble getting to sleep that night? But we didn't sleep long. 7 Shortly after midnight Joseph awakened me. He said, "Mary, quick, get up. We must leave right now. We must get out of here while the entire town is asleep." 8 "Joseph, what are you talking about?" was my sleepy reaction. He said, "I just had a dream. In it, an angel of the Lord told me to take you and Jesus and flee to Egypt. He warned me we would not be safe anywhere in Israel. We are not to tell a soul we are leaving." He was upset as he told me the terrible news that Herod would in fact soon be looking for Jesus to kill him.

9 I really reacted negatively to Joseph telling me he had a dream. I said, "Why do we have to leave at this ungodly hour? I am not going. Even Herod won't be that cruel, as to kill a small child." Joseph insisted and I strongly resisted. 10 Finally, he said to me, "Mary, time and again I have given in to what you want and how you want it. But this time, I am going to refuse to do as you want. We are leaving and we are leaving now. I have the donkey hitched to the cart. I have put a few of our things on it. I didn't have room for many. I did leave room for you and Jesus to ride in the cart." 11 "But Joseph, we don't have the money to travel anywhere, let along all the way to Egypt." With an exasperated looked he said, "Mary, Mary, do you so soon forget the riches the Magi gave us? We have plenty of money. The Lord has provided. Come, we must be going. And I mean it." 12 I was not pleased with his harshness, but I was obedient and we left within a matter of minutes. By morning we were far from Bethlehem. We were certain no

one saw us depart. 13 We knew it would be at least another day before the Magi would be telling Herod where we lived, and by that time we would be a long ways from Bethlehem. 14 We had no idea the Magi had been warned in a dream not to return to Herod. Several weeks later, we heard that about ten days after we left Bethlehem, Herod sent a band of soldiers to search for Jesus. 15 We were well known throughout the community, and many knew of our baby Jesus. However, no one had any idea what had happened to us. 16 It is ironic that our fleeing to save one child resulted in the death of dozens of others. Herod had his men kill every boy child two years of age and under in Bethlehem and the surrounding area. 17 He naturally thought we would still be somewhere in the area. Through his wicked plan to kill all the baby boys in and around Bethlehem, he believed he would be sure to kill the supposed baby King. 18 He must have felt he was so clever. I wondered how he could be so cruel. It never crossed his mind that we had fled all the way to Egypt.

19 As far as anyone in Bethlehem knew, we were a very poor family, and thus couldn't travel far from home. Neither Herod, nor anyone else, could have ever imagined the Magi had made us rich. 20 I am sure you can understand how I wept bitter tears over my friends and their toddlers Jesus had played with who had been murdered by a wicked tyrant. Also, I have often thought of the young soldiers who had to slaughter innocent baby boys. 21 Surely having to do this brutal act must have haunted at least some of them for the rest of their lives. And all because of a wicked king who had only a few more years to live and to reign. And even more ironic is that all of this slaughter was an effort to kill the one through whom life more abundant and eternal was made possible.

22 Can you believe, it was not until after the crucifixion of Jesus that I became aware of Jeremiah's prophecy? It warned, *"A voice was heard in Ramah, weeping and great mourning, Rachel weeping for the children, and she refused to be comforted, because they were no more."* I also learned that a prophet had foretold, *"Out of Egypt I called my Son."* We were living life as best we could at the time, while at the same time in such a way as to protect our baby. **23** Prophecy in regard to what we did was the furthest thing from our minds. Joseph never knew of these connections with ancient scripture. He had been dead several years prior to their being shown to me.

24 I have often wished we would have known about these prophecies at the time the events were taking place. But then it probably would not have made a great difference. We still would have done what seemed the best thing to do at the moment. **25** God does work in mysterious ways, and even common folk like us are often part of the fulfilling of His plan. And, most of the time, we are not even remotely aware we are part of His larger plan. Usually we think what we are doing is simply the result of a combination of circumstances surrounding us at the moment. **26** It is hard for us to grasp that all the events may very well be in the overall plan of the God of our fathers for us and others around us.

27 Herod lived for nearly four years after we left Bethlehem. God told Joseph in a dream when he was dead, and that we could now take Jesus back to Israel. Although we did not depart abruptly, as we did from Bethlehem, it was only a few days later until we were heading back to Israel. **28** I was so excited. You must realize neither my parents, nor any other of our relatives or friends, had seen Jesus. He was now an active, fast-growing child. His baby years were gone forever. **29** Our plan was to return and live in Bethlehem. We really liked the little town during the year and a half we lived there after the birth of Jesus. 30 We liked the thought of being near Zacharias and Elizabeth. Joseph could get his old job back. We could buy a nice home with the money the Magi had given Jesus. Joseph's father and mother were dead, and he had no close relatives in the Nazareth area. So we had no pressing reason to return to Nazareth. 31 However, Joseph heard that Archelaus, Herod's son, was now reigning over Judea and he was afraid to go there. Further, he was warned in a dream not to go to Judea, but to the Galilee area. 32 This is what influenced us to go back to Nazareth. My parents were thrilled to see us. They adored little Jesus. 33 He quickly learned to love and to take advantage of my parents as they were truly doting grandparents. I have often thought of how proud Joseph's deceased parents would have been of Jesus.

34 Here again, it was after the death of Jesus when it was pointed out to me that a prophet had spoken of us living in Nazareth, and he said Jesus would be called a Nazarene. 35 I have no idea how many other incidents in the life of Jesus have been foretold by prophets of old. I now feel there must be a lot of them. It is interesting to me that Matthew does refer to a number of them in his account of the life of Jesus. 36 I don't know how he became aware of them, but I must say the ones he refers to sure seem to fit the many situations in the life of Jesus. But, foretold by prophets or not, we had some very trying years. In all fairness, I must say that in Nazareth we also had some very pleasant and wonderful ones.

Chapter 11

ॐॐ

1 Overall, our years in Nazareth turned out to be very good ones. Jesus was getting to the point where, even though still young, he was a great help to Joseph in the carpenter shop. Between old customers, and new ones, Joseph's business was thriving again. 2 We didn't need to use any of the Magi treasures given to Jesus. It was interesting to Joseph and me that Jesus never wanted any of this wealth. 3 When we brought up the topic, he always responded, 'you just keep it'. This, more than once, turned out to be an unexpected blessing for us.

4 One nice thing about being in Nazareth was that we got to go for Passover each year in Jerusalem. 5 Jesus gave us a scare when he was twelve years old. Our entire family had gone to Jerusalem for Passover. A number of relatives and friends went together as a caravan. The children enjoyed each other's company. 6 The journey was made more pleasant because of this intimate time with family members, relatives, and friends. We were a large and joyous group of travelers. 7 A frightening thing happened near the end of our first day on our way home. We discovered Jesus was not with us. We frantically checked with others in the group and none of them remembered seeing him since shortly after we left for home. My heart almost stopped. 8 Had some evil befallen him? When he

was a baby, a wicked ruler wanted to kill him. Now, as a lad, had some harm come his way? I had always been very protective of him, but on this day I just took for granted he was with some of his playmates. 9 I knew he started the day with us. How did he get separated from us? I was frantic with fear. I began blaming Joseph and myself for not checking on him from time to time throughout the day. 10 I knew deep in my heart there was no excuse for our neglecting Jesus. My burning question was, "Will we ever find him alive?"

11 Even though it would soon be dark, Joseph and I, along with three friends, headed back to Jerusalem to try to find him. We checked with every group we met along the way. None had seen a lost young lad. 12 Finally, in Jerusalem we spent a restless night at an inn. Early the next morning, we began to search throughout the city. 13 We asked shopkeepers as well as travelers on the streets. No one had seen a young boy who appeared lost. I think we covered every street of the city, but no Jesus. 14 On the third day, we went to the Temple for prayer to try to find some peace of mind in the midst of our growing despair. Lo, and behold, there was Jesus! 15 He was talking with a group of the religious leaders. We couldn't believe our eyes, while at the same time feeling the heavy weight of despair lifted. 16 Of course, I ran up and embraced him. Even though I was so relieved, I found it difficult to contain my anger at what he had done. 17 I sternly said to him, "Son, why have you done this to me and your father? We have been desperately searching for you these three days." 18 He calmly looked at me and said, "Mother, don't you realize I must be about my Father's business." My jaw dropped in stunned disbelief. Jesus had never defied us before. I sternly said, "I sure do realize it, and so does your father. The business will need your help more than ever now that we have been

delayed three days in getting back to Nazareth." 19 I will never forget that look of deep wonderment he gave me. He didn't say anything, but his look has haunted me throughout the years. I thought, "Don't you realize how you are neglecting Joseph?"

20 Before I could start asking him the many questions on my mind, one of the religious leaders said to me. "Lady, is this your son?" 21 "Yes, he is." Looking at Joseph, he said, "And, is this his father?" I said, "Yes," and then said, "Sort of." He gruffly said, "Sort of? What do you mean sort of? Is he or isn't he the father?" 22 I hesitantly responded, "Well, yes and no." "Lady, this is too confusing for me. All I want you to know is this young man needs good sound teaching from his parents about our sacred traditions. And he needs that teaching to start immediately. 23 He is still very young and teachable. If you don't rein him in now, he is in for big trouble in the future. 24 We Temple priests have spent a lot of time with him the last couple of days. We just thought he was one of the local children. We had no idea he was from Nazareth, as you have told us. 25 We have sure found out a lot about what he believes concerning the religious life. He is strangely spiritual, but almost rebellious against our law and traditions. 26 Mark my word, he is going to be a big problem for you, and for a lot of other people, if he keeps thinking and explaining religious things as he did with us. We don't want him around the Temple anymore. The way he thinks could upset everything around here." 27 That was the end of our conversation with the religious leaders with whom Jesus had been asking and answering questions. Our one aim was to get home, and to get there as fast as we could.

28 I immediately began to again scold him, and to ask many questions. "Where did you sleep? What have you had to eat? Weren't you afraid at night? Didn't you realize how

worried we would be when you came up missing?" 29 He
didn't respond directly to any of them. He did obediently
listen. He did say at one point that his Father had taken care
of everything. I blurted out, "But how has your father taken
care of you?" He never responded. I already knew Joseph
hadn't helped him, because he never even knew where he
was. 30 He sure didn't look exhausted, and he said he
wasn't hungry when I offered him some bread. 31 I guess he
thought I had pressed him enough for answers, because he did
ask me one question. It seemed to end our discussion about
the how and why of things. He said, "Mother, do you believe
in angels?" 32 What was I to say? We left it at that and had an
otherwise uneventful journey home. I was just relieved he
was unharmed.

33 It was days later when it hit me: His Father's business!
The Temple and religious leaders talking with him! How did I
fail to understand him that day when he spoke of being about
his Father's business? 34 I then realized Jesus understood far
beyond what we had ever told him about his birth and
purpose in life. Of course, he was talking about God. It was
not Joseph. 35 But we had such a normal family life, and
Jesus being special had moved to the background of our
thinking. 36 I had gotten over considering him as someone
unusual. He was just one of our children. Certainly, through
the years, his brothers and sisters didn't think he was special.
They did feel at times he was too religious for his own good.
37 What he was trying to tell me was he was doing God's
business. No wonder Joseph and I had a strange spiritual
feeling when we found him, even in the midst of our anxiety
and fear. 38 Later, Joseph and I discussed how at the Temple
we had encountered a spiritual presence when we came upon
young Jesus. But we never really grasped this at the time. Our
worries had drowned out our real moments of worship of the
true God. Even as an aged woman, I wonder if I will ever
learn to be really aware of God's presence all the time?

Chapter 12

❧❧

1 In the carpenter shop, Jesus was a diligent and very capable worker. The customers all liked him. Many individuals told Joseph that he had a very fine son. They sometimes would remark how Jesus would be able to carry on the business. We had no doubt he could and would. 2 However, in his mid-twenties he became more withdrawn. He began to take less and less interest in the business. I became concerned about the fact he often had that faraway look. It was as if he were daydreaming, or off in another world of his own. 3 Other members in the family sensed this also. They just thought he was peculiar and let it go at that. I knew something drastic was soon going to happen. I sure didn't know what or how. 4 Joseph and I heeded the advice of the elders at the Temple, and spent a lot of time diligently and faithfully teaching Jesus about our religious traditions. There was no question he knew the law, and that he sought to keep it. 5 He was very faithful to synagogue services, and seemed to be unable to get enough of religious teaching. He was just different. 6 I couldn't escape pondering in my heart how he would save the nation from their sins. Weren't the priests doing that? How was he to add to what they were doing? 7 Every once in awhile I would even let my imagination run wild and wonder when he would be King of Israel. 8 I had no answers within me

for all of my questions. I sure wasn't going to start asking others for any answers in these areas. I didn't want to start trouble, or lead people to start thinking strange things about me and my son, Jesus.

9 Your devoted father died when Jesus was twenty-eight. I thought my heart would break. I felt at the time this was the worst thing which could ever happen to me. Little did I suspect what lay ahead. 10 The immediate months after Joseph's death, Jesus assumed much more responsibility for the business. Still, without his father's involvement, our income dropped. I found myself, from time to time, using some of the wealth the Magi had given Jesus. 11 Nevertheless, it was a great comfort to me to have Jesus in charge of the business. I felt rather secure, but in a way, I didn't. It seemed to me his heart was not really interested in being a carpenter the rest of his life. 12 Although my loss of Joseph was painful beyond words, as long as I had Jesus with me, I felt everything would work out fine. Yet, at the same time, I had a strange inward feeling things were going to change. I sure didn't know how. 13 I got some comfort in being aware of the fact Jesus was able to deal with difficult problems and situations and solve them one way or another. He was amazing in this regard. 14 This really became evident the night we were all at a wedding feast. I am sure you remember it, but I'll remind you of the details. 15 Rather early in the evening, the word spread they had run out of wine. Now folk had consumed just enough wine that they were getting unruly and demanding more. I overheard some of the servants discussing their crises. 16 One of them expressed the feeling of all of them when he asked his buddies, "What are we going to do?" I happened to overhear his question.

17 I don't know why, but the thought came to me that Jesus could somehow solve this problem. He knew a lot of

winemakers, as they were his customers. I told the servant
to go to him, and ask for help. I did emphasize that he
should do whatever Jesus told him to do. He was not to
question him, even though his suggestion might be a little
far out. 18 I thought he might send them to wine dealers in
the area, even though it was beyond their ordinary closing
time. I never dreamed his suggestion would be as
outrageous as it was. Jesus told them to fill six thirty-gallon
jars with water. 19 They looked questionably at me, but I
just nodded approval and mouthed, "Do it." I sure didn't
know why, but I trusted Jesus. 20 It took a while, but they
filled them all. Then Jesus said, "Now take a cup of it from
the jar to the host." The servant said, "No way am I going
to take a cup of water to the host." Jesus spoke again, and
there was no doubt he wanted the host to taste what was in
the jars. 21 And there was no mistaking he wanted a cup
taken to the host, and taken now. Honestly, I was
embarrassed. Take water to the host? This will really get
him and the crowd upset. 22 But I kept my mouth shut.
Frankly, I was surprised the servant took the cup full to the
host. I can assure you he was not too happy about doing so.
23 I was fully unprepared for what followed. The servant
came back so excited he could hardly contain himself. He
said the host took a drink of it, and then asked him, "Why
did you save the best wine for last? This is excellent! 24 I
have never tasted any better wine in all my life. Why have
you done this? You know it is not as I would have wanted.
You are well aware we always serve the best first, and then
the wine of lesser quality." 25 But he settled down, and
announced to all there was plenty of wine available. He
urged them to continue to drink and to enjoy themselves.

26 This was the first miracle Jesus did. No one was
more startled than me. Water into wine! Unbelievable! But
I was there. I witnessed it happening. It certainly was the

topic on the lips of practically everyone in the area for many days. 27 Yes, I know stories have gotten out that Jesus miraculously repaired toys even as a child. Such rumors are absolutely false. He had never done any miracle prior to the wine incident. 28 Further, you must realize neither Joseph, myself, nor any of your brothers and sisters, ever dreamed he would perform spectacular miracles.

29 Here is an almost laughable thing which happened following the wedding. After hearing of how the wine became available from the water filled jars, the host perceived there must be some magical power in the jars. So he instructed them to be locked away in a special room. 30 Some weeks later he had another big banquet. He instructed his servants to bring out the jars and to fill them with water. 31 This they did. He took a sip. It was still water! He never did seem to realize it was not the jars, but Jesus, that made the difference. Jesus was the reason for the miracle, and not the jars. 32 It is so hard for folk to perceive spiritual power. We heard later he kept the jars and tried it a couple more times, but of course, the water remained water. I have no idea what ultimately became of those six jars made famous by Jesus.

Chapter 13

❧

1 Jesus was about thirty years old when we got word that Elizabeth's son, John, had become a famous prophet. John, in his adult years, left home and lived in the desert. They say his food was mainly locust. 2 He came roaring out of the desert, boldly preaching that people should repent. Large crowds went out to hear him. He turned many of them back to God. 3 He told the common people that true repentance would involve giving to the poor. Those who had two coats were to give one to a person who had none. 4 He told the tax collectors to collect only the actual tax, and not to cheat the taxpayers. He also told the Roman soldiers not to forcefully take money from people, or to falsely accuse people, and to be content with their wages. 5 So many people repented and were baptized. He soon became known as John the Baptist. John thought it very interesting that none of the religious leaders asked how they should show repentance. It seemed they came simply to listen, to criticize, and to check on what was happening.

6 One day Jesus said to me. "Mother, it is time I leave. I must go and hear John. My call is now upon me. My brothers are old enough to care for the business. And don't worry about me. I will be alright." 7 The day he left to hear John was the last time he was to be home for any length of time. He was on his mission. I felt very much alone even

though you other six children were with me.

8 I was told when John saw Jesus coming toward him, he cried out, "Behold the Lamb of God who takes away the sin of the world." Little did he know my firstborn would end up being slaughtered, and his shed blood be the atonement for the world. 9 Jesus asked John to baptize him. John was hesitant, but finally consented to do so. The word is that when Jesus came up out of the water, the Holy Spirit descended on him in the form of a dove. I was told those present actually saw this manifestation of the Spirit. 10 People insist they heard a voice out of heaven. It was like thunder, and yet they understood it. The Father proclaimed, "This is my beloved son, in whom I am well pleased." 11 It was then that reality crossed my mind. It became clear to me that now he truly was about his Father's business. This was the beginning of things unheard of in all Israel. 12 Weeks went by and I heard no more about, or from, Jesus. Then one day he showed up for a short visit. I could hardly believe my eyes. He was so thin and gaunt. I cried out, "My son, what has happened to you?" His reply was everything was alright. 13 "Where have you been and what have you been doing? Come, I must prepare a big meal for you. You look half starved." He politely said, "No, Mother! No big meal. Just give me a few vegetables." 14 He was much more talkative then usual about himself. He told me that after being baptized by John, he was led of the Spirit into the wilderness to be tested by the devil. 15 He thought he would be there only a few days. It ended up being nearly six weeks. He related how he had nothing to eat during the entire time. Now I realized why he looked so thin and was so weak. 16 He said there was a stream nearby and so he did have water. We talked all afternoon. I was intrigued with how he thought the attacks of Satan were so personal. 17 It was evident he sensed this to be a time of real testing. But it

seemed he had never conceived it would be so personal and powerful. **18** He said he was very hungry after the first three days. It was then Satan tempted him by saying, "If you be the son of God, turn some stones into bread to eat." **19** Jesus responded, "Life was more than eating. Life also consists of knowing and understanding the words of God." He explained to Satan that God's words are the real bread of life.

20 I have never gone days without food. I felt Jesus must be famished. He told me he wasn't hungry. He said after about three days his hunger pains disappeared. This seemed strange to me, but he assured me it was true. **21** He went on to say some days later Satan took him to the top of the steeple of the Temple in Jerusalem. **22** There the devil tried to get him to believe he would be treated very special if he were the son of God. Satan told Jesus to jump, and the angels would catch him. I was touched when he said, "Now, Mother, I believe in angels and their help, but I also know a person should not tempt the Lord. I told the devil this in no uncertain terms." **23** Some days later, he was amazed how the devil showed him the kingdoms of this world, and sought to make a deal with him. **24** Satan told him if he would worship him, he would give him all the kingdoms of this world. Jesus said it would include a lot of wealth and fame. But he knew deep in his heart a person should only worship the true and living God. **25** I knew it was wrong and I didn't mention it to him, but at the time, I thought this was his chance to be king not only of the Jews, but of the world. I had never been able to get out of my mind the Magi had called him the King of the Jews.

26 It may be because of my poor background, but I would sometimes think it would be great to be the mother of a King. But, that is enough of my foolish thoughts. **27.** I did ask him how he responded to Satan's promise. He replied that he told him a person should worship only the Lord Almighty. **28** This last onslaught of Satan ended their encounters. Jesus told me Satan then left him. He assured me he knew Satan would be back to tempt him in other ways. He emphasized that Satan never quits trying to get a person to turn from God.

29 After he had shared all these things with me, I mentioned I had some bad news for him. It was then I told him John was in prison. His plain and powerful preaching had gotten him into trouble. **30** Jesus asked, "But, Mother, what is his crime?" I told him John had committed no crime. His problem was he had publicly condemned Herod for taking his brother Phillip's wife, to be his wife. John bluntly preached this was wrong. **31** John's imprisonment deeply troubled Jesus. A few days later, he told me he had a mission to fulfill. He left without telling me where he was going, or what he would be doing. I thought he might go into seclusion for a few weeks. It was obvious he realized he could not preach the truth to or about the religious. Really, I was concerned as to what he might keep teaching. **32** On several occasions, he had said to me, a person should do as the religious ones taught, not as they lived. I knew if he taught this publicly, he would be in big trouble. I never suspected he was about to launch his public ministry.

33 Several days later, I learned from friends he had began to gather a group of disciples to travel with him and to be willing to be taught by him. **34** He was never home again for any length of time. There were times when he was in the area. Salome and I would go to hear him teach, and to witness miracles by the laying on of his hands. **35** By the way, John never did get out of prison. He was beheaded. The daughter of Herod's wife, Herodias, danced as the entertainment at Herod's birthday party. He was so pleased, he offered her up to half of his kingdom. **36** She asked her mother what she should ask of Herod. Herodias seized on this opportunity to get rid of John. She told her daughter to ask Herod for John's head on a platter. How can you possibly get more cruel than this? 37 In a way, I was glad Elizabeth and Zacharias were both dead. They did not have to live through the agony of knowing their son had been beheaded. 38 Little did I realize, at the time, the agony I would have to endure, as I witnessed my son, Jesus, being crucified between the two criminals.

Chapter 14

જ⊷ન

1 Sometimes I have the feeling it would have been better if I had died as a much younger woman. Life has not been easy for me. I have had many problems, heartaches, and disappointments. One of my many disappointments was the fact Jesus chose just ordinary people to be his disciples. 2 You could safely say I was disappointed regarding all of them. They were all unlearned men. Of course, none of them had a deep religious knowledge background. Some insisted Matthew was well educated. This may be true, but he was a hated tax collector. I didn't really trust him.

3 Another thing which really perplexed me was when Jesus started to teach, preach, and heal in the Galilee area. For the life of me, I couldn't understand why he didn't start in Jerusalem. My question was: "Who in the world had ever heard of the land of Zabulon or the land of Nephthalim?" 4 I felt that if he were to be teaching about religion, why not do so among the religious people? Most of the people living where he began his public ministry were Gentiles. In addition, there were no large cities in the area. 5 In spite of this, huge crowds would gather to hear him teach. He usually would heal many of them. Really, it was evident his miracles drew the crowds even more than his teaching. Of course, the people loved him and what he

taught and did. 6 It took about a year for the news to spread widely about Jesus. He had a somewhat obscure first year, but he became very popular during his second year. 7 Rumors began to spring up he should be made a king. I never heard of him encouraging such a thing, but I thought maybe what the Magi had said would now come true. But my dreams of Jesus being king were soon ended. After a little over two years of public preaching, teaching, and healing, opposition began to develop. And, I mean intense opposition.

8 The more the common people followed Jesus, the more a small segment of the religious community seemed to hate him. Most of the Pharisees and the Sadducees were really incensed by him. I heard they were even planning to kill him. 9 Why, oh why, would they want to kill one who healed and helped so many? I found it very difficult not to worry about him. One day when he had stopped by the house, I asked him why he had not done any of these wonderful healings while he was still living at home. 10 His answer really puzzled me. He said, "Mother, I am not really doing these miracles in my own power. The power of the Spirit is doing them. I am simply the vessel the Holy Spirit is choosing to flow through to defeat the onslaught of Satan, which often results in sickness." 11 He went on to say, "I know the Holy Spirit came upon you, and I was born without an earthly father. But do you realize I permitted my coming to earth to happen?" 12 This really shocked me. I blurted out, "How could someone that didn't even live permit something to happen?" He became very serious and said, "Mother, you just don't understand." He seemed a little troubled. After a long silence, he said, "I want to share some important truths with you. 13 In my frequent quiet times alone with the Father, he has told me many things. Among them being that He had asked me to come to earth

and I agreed. 14 You see, in the completely spiritual world, I am the Son of God. Really, I am the I Am. When with the Father, I never was or never will be. I am. It is not I was or I will be. It is just I am. 15 He sent me to earth through the power of the Spirit using you as the earthly vessel. You see, Mother, since I was willing to be emptied of all my heavenly powers, I don't have any more available power than any other man. Yes, I willingly agreed to empty myself of all Godly power and to become a human being. 16 You must understand, I am not half God and half man. I am all human. It wasn't until after my baptism that the Holy Spirit fell upon me and entered into my spirit. It was then I was really able to teach and heal with power. 17 The Holy Spirit is my source of power. I cannot do or teach anything without the approval of my Father and the power of the Holy Spirit. 18 As a man, I believe, and then God does his part. He honors my believing. I am trying to get people to understand that, regardless of one's status in life, if you really believe, great things can happen. I want them to realize extraordinary things can happen through ordinary people and ordinary things. 19 My Father wants me, and everyone else, to believe Him. This is where so many of the children of Israel are widely missing the mark. Their traditions and teachings are focused upon pleasing the Father, instead of simply and purely believing the Father. 20 There is no way anyone can really please the Father by doing something for Him, or sacrificing something to Him. He is perfect. Therefore He has everything He now needs, or ever will need. 21 Trying to please Him through animal or grain sacrifices, prayers, fasting, sitting in sackcloth and ashes, or just trying to be and do good alone cannot really please Him. What He wants is for you to believe Him. 22 Abraham came close to this truth, but ceremonies and keeping rigid laws of behavior still won the day. Moses even wrote that

Abraham believed God and it was counted to him as righteousness. The powerful truth of the power of believing has practically been abandoned and replaced by ritual and regulations."

23 He saw I was getting a bit overwhelmed with what he was trying to explain to me. So he said, "Mother, let me tell you plainly what I am trying to teach. I know you are aware of the strong opposition I am having to my teaching spiritual truths." 24 He then gave me examples as to why the religious leaders were so angry at him. He said, "For instance, they are very put out with my teaching concerning repentance. They stress repentance as being sorry for some deed a person has done, and then making some sacrifice to atone for it. 25 The truth is simply that true repentance is much deeper. You must realize the most important repenting anyone can do is to repent from believing God doesn't love them. 26 Mother, do you realize how our religious leaders look down on the poor, the Gentiles, the uneducated, and others who do not do as they think they should? They feel a person must know the details of the law and perfectly keep and observe these hundreds of regulations. 27 My Father asked me to come into the world, because He loves the world. He isn't impressed with litany, liturgy, feasts, or sacrifices. 28 Many of the prophets have taught this truth about believing the Father, but the priesthood continues to stress the sacrifices and keeping the minute details of the law. I don't agree with this approach. It is not right. And I want all to know it is not what my Father desires.

29 "One of the reasons I started teaching in the Galilean region was to convey, in action, as well as word, that God loves Gentiles as much as He loves Jews. Most of those living in that area are Gentiles. 30 Truly, I was anointed by the Holy Spirit to preach the good news of the Father's love

to the poor and to heal the sick, regardless of nationality.
31 I have been anointed by the Holy Spirit to be a light in a
land of darkness. In a sense, both Jews and Gentiles are
walking in darkness. The Gentiles, because all they have
heard through the generations is God doesn't, and never
will, love them. The Jews, because they feel their having
favor with God means they are the only ones the Father
loves. 32 They have failed to grasp that their being favored
of God really means being the ones chosen to bring the
Father's message of love to everyone. It means realizing
the Father is no respecter of persons, and He wants
individuals anywhere, and everywhere, to believe Him.
33 The religious leaders feel their high calling is to preserve
Jewish tradition. It is obvious to me this means a way of
preserving and maintaining their jobs and status. The
opposition to me is from those who feel that if people
follow my teaching their place of power and wealth will be
eliminated. They would rather keep people in darkness than
lose their position. What a tragedy. 34 I love everybody.
And I always teach my Father loves everyone, regardless of
what the religious may think or do. One of the things I am
continually teaching my disciples is to go into the whole
world and preach the good news of the Father's love. 35 I
am trying to get them to understand their wealth and time
should be devoted to telling the good news of the Father's
love. 36 The religious ones spend practically all of their
efforts continually telling each other the good news over
and over. This lifestyle shuts people out from the Father's
love. It is not a lifestyle with which the Father is pleased.
37 My teaching and lifestyle brings to all people the
message that the Father loves them, and they should turn to
Him. Let me tell you what I mean about sacred selfishness
and how it is so cruel.

38 "You should have heard the uproar when word spread

that I had chosen the tax collector, Matthew, to be one of my disciples. His being chosen caused an even bigger uproar when he held a huge banquet and invited not only fellow tax collectors, but a lot of poor people, and even harlots off the streets. 39 I loved what he is doing and I am most willing to attend the banquet. It gives me a great opportunity to teach that the Father loves everyone, and anyone can claim Him as their Father. 40 Matthew has become the most zealous disciple as far as trying to get others to hear my teaching, and to believe what I taught. He has held many such banquets, and I have willingly gone to all of them. 41 The religious keep condemning me, as well as Matthew, and those who attend his banquets. I love that Matthew always invites a lot of individuals who will never be able to return the favor of a banquet for him. They are truly poor people." 42 I was so pleased Jesus was sharing so much with me. He went on to say, "Here is an incident that is almost laughable. I was entering Jericho and a large crowd was gathering. 43 Several feet ahead of me, I noticed a man climbing a tree. I presumed it was to get a better look at what was going on. I asked who he was and was told he was Zacchaeus, the most hated tax collector in the area. 44 When I arrived near the tree, I looked up and said to him, "Zacchaeus come down, because I want to go to your house for dinner." My, oh my, the crowd erupted in disbelief and opposition. They couldn't believe I was really aware of how sinful the man was with whom I was planning to have dinner. They were really upset." 45 I asked Jesus how things went at the dinner. He said. "Zacchaeus is a very small man in stature, but one with a brilliant mind and big heart. He was so touched by my paying attention to him, and being willing to come to his home. I was amazed how many he had invited to the dinner. It was a big affair. 46 He really seemed to be sincerely interested and deeply moved inwardly with what I taught throughout dinner. I told all who were present that the Father loved everyone and wanted to help them. 47 I stressed how the Father wants individuals to believe Him. I also emphasized and spent some time teaching how the Father especially wants us to help the poor. Zacchaeus really seemed intrigued with this. He asked me, 'What happens if a person doesn't help the poor?' 48 I told him if one doesn't help the poor they will be cast into the lake of fire. His countenance changed as if this seemed to hit him hard. I kept teaching about other things. 49 All of a sudden he blurted out, 'Jesus, I am going to give half of my money to the poor.' Then he said, 'And if I have robbed anyone, I will repay him fourfold.' I thought to myself, this very rich man is soon to be a lot poorer. However, he will be greatly blessed in other ways."

50 Jesus continued with, "Let me give you one more instance where I tried to show that the Father loves everyone. Several of the leading Jewish men brought to me a married woman. Her husband was unaware of her life as a prostitute. He found out about her double life and was now demanding she be stoned. Several of the men were most willing to join him in doing this. 51 They said she should be stoned to death. This beautiful young woman was really frightened. She knew what her end would be. 52 Our traditions are so strong, she even believed she deserved being stoned. It has always bothered me how the man involved in an affair with such a woman is never held guilty or punished. 53 I wanted her to experience the Father's love and forgiveness. I knelt on the sand and wrote the words, 'you have abused her'. I anticipated the men would be curious as to what I had written. Sure enough, in a few moments, one came up to look. I wrote his name in the sand under the statement, 'you have abused her'. 54 He sure didn't linger. Another was right there to look and I

wrote his name. There were three others who came to look. I wrote their names under the other ones. They immediately turned and quickly went back to the group. 55 I heard them talking excitedly among themselves. It was then I heard the sound of a stone hitting the ground. I heard another thud of a dropped stone, and another, and then several of them all at once. 56 A few minutes later, I looked up and they were all gone. Evidently every one of them had abused her at one time or another. They sure didn't want their name written by me. 56 As far as they knew, I would leave it in the sand for some time. Others would be able to see their names. That was something they surely did not want. They just wanted the woman killed. With her dead, there would never be a witness to their sin. 57 I said to the young woman, 'Where are your accusers, who accuse you no more?' She meekly said they all just hurried away. 58 Then I said to her, 'I don't hold anything against you, nor does the Father. God loves you.' This startled her. I went on to say to her that I certainly didn't condemn her. I told her to go and sin no more. I then told her, 'God wants to help you, and will help you live a life that is good for you and others.' 59 Her husband stood there in startled disbelief. He just couldn't believe I was being so kind to a woman taken in adultery. It sure touched him that I had forgiven her. It was evident he forgave her also. My heart was touched as she and her husband happily departed hand-in-hand. They really grasped the truth I was imparting. 60 Her accusers missed the truth entirely. They never got the point that I was condemning them, not her. They just continued to condemn me for preaching heresy and forgiving an adulterous woman. And I am just as sure they found another woman of the street for their own sensual pleasure."

Chapter 15

❧❧

1 Jesus went on to say, "But it gets even more interesting. A second thing I teach concerning the repentance the Father desires is that you should repent from believing God does not want to help you. The religious ones really come against me for this type of teaching. 2 Yes, I definitely teach regardless of who you are, or what your situation may be, God wants to help you. It almost drives them insane when I constantly teach God wants to help everyone. 3 Then they really lose it when, by healing people, I seek to prove the truth of God wanting to help everyone. I have even healed many people who are not of Israel. 4 The religious leaders really got upset with my healing of a Roman Centurion's servant. Yet, that Centurion had more faith than any I have seen in all Israel. 5 Then there was the daughter of the Syro-Phoenician woman who was healed. This was a stumbling block for them, because she was a Gentile. But I just keep marching on, healing and helping people. 6 I have instructed my disciples to do the same thing. I have not only taught them to do it, I have sent them out to heal the sick and demon possessed. One day I sent seventy of them out, two-by-two, to heal the sick. They were absolutely amazed at what happened. 7 They could hardly believe just ordinary men, as they were, could do such extraordinary things. They realized even the devils were subject to them

as they believed. I then told them this was great, but spiritual matters were most important. I know healings attract crowds, but believing is what brings one into the right relationship with the Father.

8 "In addition to the healings, I often do some very tangible things to help people. One really outstanding instance of this was when I fed over five thousand men, plus women and children, from just a few loaves and fishes." 9 This sounded almost too astounding for me. I hesitantly asked Jesus, "But how did you bake all that bread and cook all the fish?" 10 He said, "The Father took care of that. All who were there were amazed the bread tasted fresh, and the fish was deliciously cooked." He never explained, and I sure never understood how the Father cooked all that food. Jesus did go on to say, "Those who were there have never ceased to talk about it." 11 I said, "They must have all believed in you and the spiritual life after witnessing such an amazing experience." 12 His response was interesting. "Mother, you would think they would have gotten the message. Would you believe, the next day they were seeking me, but not for spiritual power and how to believe for miracles. No, they wanted more bread and fish. It is a constant battle to get individuals to believe. Most of them just want to receive.

13 "The third thing I teach about repentance is the one thing that really makes the religious ones so angry. I teach, and truly believe, that religion cannot save you. You are saved by believing and not by laws, long prayers, rote attendance at religious services, or festivals. 14 The religious traditionally teach, and sincerely believe, that what you don't do makes you right in the sight of God. I teach it is what you believe and do which produces the right relationship with God. 15 They have been very troubled with the fact that some have correctly said I live a

sinless life. They point out how I often sin. One of my sins, from their point of view, is sometimes I fail to wash my hands properly before meals. Another gross sin from their standpoint is I associate with the poor and outcasts. 16 They teach, and demand, observance of their hundreds of rules and regulations of the law. I have tried to convey to them there are only two laws which are really important. These two essential ones override all the others. 17 The first is that you should love the Lord your God with all your heart, mind, and soul. The second is you should love your neighbor as yourself. These two essentials outweigh all their hundreds of rules and regulations which have evolved through the centuries. 18 Believe me when I say I keep these two essential laws. I do not break them. Therefore, I do not commit sin. I readily admit I have sinned according to man-made laws. But this is no problem with my Father. It really honors Him."

19 It was becoming evident to Jesus that what he was saying was beginning to trouble me. He then began to try to comfort me. He stressed I should not worry about him. 20 I tried to get him to stay home for several weeks. This would provide time for things to quiet down. Then he could once again teach and heal throughout the land. 21 I reminded him of what the Temple leader had said when he was twelve years old. I asked him if he remembered what it was. He said, "I sure do. How could I ever forget?" 22 I sternly stressed what we had been warned about years ago, that he would be seen as a troublemaker, and now it seemed to be coming to pass. I urged him to back off a little, and let things work out peacefully. 23 His response was he just couldn't be unfaithful to his high calling. He said he had to do what he was doing, and that he was most willing to suffer the consequences. 24 He realized I was being overwhelmed and changed the subject. We talked about

family for awhile longer. We then had dinner and shortly afterwards went to bed. I didn't sleep much that night. He left early the next morning. That was the last time Jesus was home.

25 Because of what happened in the weeks that followed, I have often regretted I had not talked with him longer that day. I have deliberately tried not to let my time with John go by without talking at length with him about Jesus. I have learned much from John. He has been such a great blessing to me. 26 No one will ever be able to take the place of your father and Jesus in my life. But I must say, John has been a tremendous help and blessing. 27 The last occasion I had any extended time alone with Jesus was his visit with us in Jerusalem during his last Passover.

Chapter 16

❧❦

1 I mentioned to the family I would like to go to the Passover several days early. I had no idea this would be Jesus' last Passover. This thought never crossed my mind. I suggested the girls go with me. You boys would come down just a couple of days before Passover. 2 There would be some relatives and friends going early and we would travel with them. I told you boys not to worry about our safety, because I knew others would be joining our group along the way. We would be glad to have them do so. 3 Sure enough, it happened. By late afternoon of our first day, there was a large group of us traveling together. I was thankful for the big strong men of some of the families. We felt very safe and secure. 4 The girls soon found several girls of their own age. They enjoyed each other's company all the way to Jerusalem. 5 I wanted to spend some days with my dear friends, Mary and Martha. I hadn't seen them for a long time. I had heard their brother Lazarus was very ill and not expected to live much longer. I was hoping we could get there before he died. He was such a wonderful man, and a very close friend of Jesus. 6 The next day, after we arrived and got settled in Jerusalem, your sisters and I went to Mary and Martha's home. We were not prepared for the surprise which awaited us. 7 I knocked on the door and a few seconds later Lazarus opened it. He was

surprised to see us and gave all three of us a hearty welcome hug. We just kept staring at him. Finally I blurted out, "Lazarus we heard you were deathly sick. You sure look healthy now. In fact, we heard you would probably be dead and buried by the time we got here." 8 He laughed and replied. "You are right. I was dead and buried before you arrived." 9. We all sort of laughed, because we thought he surely must be kidding us. We certainly didn't know what to say. 10 Then he became more serious and said, "You think I am joking, don't you?" By this time Mary and Martha had come into the room and greeted us. They urged us to sit down and relax. 11 Then Lazarus said, "Let me tell you the whole story. I did die. I was buried." "You what! You died, and were buried?" loudly stammered Salome. "I don't believe it! You've got to be kidding!" 12 Lazarus responded, "No, I am not kidding and I am not trying to tease you. I truly did die. In fact, I was in the tomb four days." The girls really got excited. They peppered him with questions. 13 "How does it feel to be dead? Did you know anything after you died? Does your brain keep working? Did you see anyone you knew who had died?" 14 Finally Lazarus said, "My dear girls, you are asking things I am asked all the time. I can say no to all of your questions so far." 15 He then went on to say, "I feel rather funny at times. Would you believe me when I say even when I walk down the street people just stop and stare at me? Many of them have known me and the family for years. They know I died and that I was buried. They know I was in the tomb four days. 16 Those who never knew me personally, but have heard about my coming back from the dead, are just as curious to see me as are my friends. 17 Believe me, because of my terrible sickness I really suffered prior to my death. Dying wasn't easy. But neither has it been easy to be back with the family. And Jesus has really become well-known since he brought me back to life. The news about this feat is spreading like wild fire. 18 I know he has had a lot of opposition from religious leaders, but I don't see how they can keep opposing him much longer. There are just too many people following him. You might say even worshiping him. 19 I hear there are nearly two million in the Jerusalem area now for the Passover. They are expecting over two and half million." 20 He switched the topic to what we found out later was one of his pet peeves. He said, "I want you to stop and think how much money the religious leaders will make this year. They will have to put their approval on at least two hundred and fifty thousand lambs. 21 And of course, the lambs will have to be obtained from shepherds they approve or they won't pronounce them worthy of sacrifice. This way they will ultimately get a kickback on all the lambs. 22 In addition, just imagine how much the money changers will make. The priests will only permit certain coins to be credited as proper to be given to the Temple. So this gives the crooks, excuse me, I mean money changers, a chance to make out like bandits at the money exchange tables."

23 Martha broke in and said, "Lazarus, stop it." He sheepishly replied, "All right, I will stop talking about the leaders. But you know yourself they are a bunch of crooks and thieves. I can't help it, but I know many others agree, feel that during Passover the Temple is more a den of thieves than a place of prayer and worship. 24 Please forget and forgive that outburst. I must get back to my being alive. But first, do you want to hear something strange? I do mean really strange? I heard the religious leaders, after I was brought back to life, immediately began to figure out a way to kill Jesus. 25 This is one of the biggest jokes I have ever heard. How do they expect to kill a man who just raised a man back to life who had been in the grave four days? They

will never be able to kill Jesus. **26** Do you realize practically all the people are following Jesus now? Everywhere he goes there are huge crowds. Recently I have been going with him. The people want to see me as much as they want to see him. Jesus is just too popular for anyone to even think of killing him. **27** One day, as there were thousands listening to him teach, I had this far out thought. I think the people may make Jesus their King, and I will end up his right hand man, and second in control." **28** Martha blurted out, "Lazarus, what are you talking about? Get this kind of thinking out of your mind. You should be ashamed of yourself for even speaking such nonsense in the presence of these young girls."

29 I can appreciate her reaction, but to be real honest, his words were making me feel better. I was beginning to think to myself that at long last Jesus will end up King of the Jews. **30** The people will crown him as King. They will bypass the religious leaders. He will become their real leader. At last I will be the mother of a King. He will be a King like King David. **31** I was brought back to reality with hearing Lazarus saying, "Mary and Martha have told me of Jesus arriving after I was dead and buried. They were frustrated by the fact he had not come earlier and healed me. They, of course, had heard of his many miracles, and had witnessed many of them."

32 "Jesus finally did arrive. But he was four days too late. The first thing he did was to calmly tell my sisters to believe. He told them I would live again. They were a little put out with his comments. They assured Jesus they believed I would live again in the resurrection of the dead. **33** Then Jesus asked to be taken to the tomb." Lazarus was getting very emotional at this point and asked Martha to continue to fill us in on the details. **34** Martha related that when they arrived at the grave Jesus didn't say much. He never even prayed for Lazarus to be restored to life. She then said, "Of course, at that moment it never crossed our minds concerning the possibility of Lazarus being brought back to life. 35 My sister and I had mixed feelings. We were comforted by having Jesus with us. At the same time, we were almost angry at him for not coming sooner and healing Lazarus. 36 After all, he traveled all over the country healing people. We had heard of at least two times when he raised people from the dead. Why, oh why, did he neglect his own very close friend? 37 Then he uttered a very brief, but moving prayer. He thanked the Father for hearing him. He went on in his prayer, saying he knew the Father heard him, but he wanted us to know the Father had sent him. At the moment, we couldn't figure out how this prayer fit into this situation. 38 All we knew for sure was we certainly understood what it meant to lose a loved one. We were sincerely grieving over our brother's death. You better believe after Lazarus came forth we sure believed Jesus was sent from God. Who else could raise a dead one like Lazarus? 39 But in that moment, we missed this point in his prayer. We were all weeping. Jesus was calm and very serious looking. All of a sudden he began to sob almost uncontrollably. It was then that everyone seemed to grasp how much he really loved Lazarus. 40 We thought he was so sorry he had failed to do what he should, and could have done. We felt regret had now hit him with full force. 41 In the days ahead, we realized he cried because all of us at the tomb were so reluctant to believe in the real presence and power of God.

42 "In the midst of all of us crying, Jesus made a surprising command to some of the men. He told them to roll the stone away. They just stood there in stunned disbelief. I cried out he would be stinking. I further said, 'Please, don't do this to us. Let him continue to lie in

peace'. 43 Jesus looked at the men with a look I will never forget. There was no way the men were not going to do his bidding after such a look. It was as if he were sternly saying, 'Get it done.' 44 Without saying a word to each other, three men stepped forward and rolled the heavy stone away. 45 The foul odor literally gushed out. It practically took our breath away. It left some of us uncontrollably coughing. We all began to hastily back away from the tomb. To our amazement Jesus took a couple of steps toward it. 46 My sister even cried out to Jesus to not go near his dead body. She pleaded with him to have the men put the stone back in place. She said, "We know his body is in there, and we should let it lie in peace." 47 Seconds later, Jesus shouted with a very loud voice, '**Lazarus, come out!**' At that moment we all thought he was crazy. The thought even flashed through our minds it may be that the authorities are right. He really is out of his mind. Maybe he is a mad man. Or worse yet, he was possessed of the devil. 48 Whatever each was thinking, most certainly our minds were racing with way-out thoughts."

49 I remember breaking in on Martha and saying, "What happened? How in the world did it work out Lazarus is here in the house today?" Martha responded with, "Mary, this is the most unbelievable thing. 50 By that time we were all staring into the open tomb. The foul odor was still there, but by then we were used to it. Our gazes and minds were all centered on the open tomb. 51 It is impossible to tell you how frightened we were when we saw Lazarus move. We couldn't believe our eyes. Later we all mentioned about the goose bumps we felt. Many of us said our hair actually stood on end. 52 Of course, we all felt we were seeing things. With the first slight movement we just thought it was a shadow from the way the light was hitting him. But then the movement became more pronounced. All of a

sudden, he was sitting up. Our mouths were wide open with amazement by this time. We absolutely could not believe it. 53 Then he stood up. Several in the group cried out in fear. Our dear next-door neighbor, who had come with us, fainted. And you won't believe one of the thoughts which crossed my mind. 54 Here is my brother coming back to life, but when he stood up and started to walk I thought about how he was going to tear the cloth. Can you believe it? I was worried about the gravecloth in the presence of Lazarus being restored to life. 55 He then began to walk, came out of the tomb and stood right there before our very eyes. We were all stunned. We became like statues as we stared at him. Jesus broke the tension by calmly saying, 'Some of you unwrap him and let him go.' Everyone was hesitant. No one stepped forward to unwrap him. 56 Jesus was a little disturbed. He rather sternly said, 'Unwrap him. Go ahead. You won't become defiled by touching a dead person. Don't you understand? He is not dead. He lives!' 57 With that, two of the men stepped forward and began unwrapping Lazarus. From the time they started to unwrap him, we all wondered what he would look like. We just kept staring. 58 We waited breathlessly for what seemed an eternity. Finally, the last of the seemingly endless length of cloth came off of his face. Our mouths dropped open in disbelief. Lazarus looked twenty years younger. And, oh, he had such a big, beautiful smile.

59 "His first words were, 'What happened? Why am I not sick anymore? And what are you all doing here?' Then he saw Jesus. That was a happy reunion. He cried out, 'Jesus, how wonderful to see you!' They gave each other a great embrace. 60 We were ready and eager to ask Lazarus a lot of questions. But before we could start asking our questions, he started asking more of his own. 'What are we all doing here in the graveyard? Why do you all look so

pale? Why do you look like you have seen a ghost or something? Why do some of you look like you are about to faint? And why am I out here with only a little cloth wrapped around my hips? Where are my clothes?' 61 He never gave us time to answer, he just kept asking questions. Finally I said, 'Lazarus, let's go back to the house. You can get into some decent clothes. We can then tell you the whole story.' 62 I asked Jesus to come with us. He said he had some things he had to do and would see us later. We never had a chance to talk with him again after that. Lazarus then broke in and told what happened back at the house. 63 He said, "I could hardly believe what Mary and Martha were telling me. I just thought I had gotten better in my sleep. I could only remember being in torturous pain, and then being so weak. Everything was blank after that until I was standing in the graveyard. I had no idea I had died, and been buried for four days. 64 I couldn't tell them a thing of what death was like, because I don't remember a thing. Let me repeat, I had no idea that I had been dead four days. And, I sure couldn't understand why I now felt so good. 65 Of course, I didn't know at that moment Jesus had just performed his greatest miracle." He then said, "Salome, you and your sister will be interested in this. Now I can't go to town, or even outside the house, without a crowd gathering around me. 66 I hear word of my death, and coming back to life, has really gotten around. And it must be true, because I sure have become a celebrity. All I had to do to become one was to die." Then he threw back his head in hearty laughter. 67 It was then it really hit us we were visiting with the Lazarus we had known through the years. I certainly felt there were better days ahead for Jesus. Now the religious people would have to accept him. The thought even crossed my mind that now they might make him King of the Jews.

68 Of course, I didn't know until Lazarus mentioned it, the religious leaders at one time sought to come up with a plan to kill Jesus. I wondered in my heart, how cruel can men be? Why are some religious people so very cruel when some of their teachings are being challenged? 69 Sad but true, Lazarus had told us correctly. We just didn't realize this truth at the moment. He laughed at their rumored scheming. I shuddered at it. Would they really kill my son?

Chapter 17

࿇࿇࿇

1 These threats temporarily upset me, but still didn't concern me too much at the time. I sincerely felt the wickedness of a few of the religious leaders could not prevail in the presence of the wide acceptance of Jesus by the people. 2 I now realize how naïve I was. I just wasn't able to grasp how the power of evil could dwell in the hearts and actions of the wicked and perverse leaders. 3 However, I was feeling better about the safety of Jesus. Up to this time, I had just about concluded the opposition from religious leaders would be the end of his ministry. 4 Now I was feeling the tide of popularity had turned, and his opposition was diminishing. It was obvious to the thousands in Jerusalem at this Passover that he was a powerful and good man. He could very well be their long promised deliverer. 5 How I wished Joseph could have been there to see how popular and famous Jesus had become. He would have been very proud of him.

6 A few days later, we were at our room in Jerusalem. The girls were outside with some of their friends. Suddenly Salome came dashing into the house yelling, "Mother, Mother, come quickly. Jesus is entering the city." 7 Someone had told her he was coming and he was going to be a King. How my heart leapt with joy. We quickly hurried out to the area where large crowds were lining the

street. 8 I imagined the beauty of the big white horse he would be on, and how majestic he would look upon it. 9 I could hear the shouts of "Hosanna, Hosanna in the highest." My heart was racing. It has finally come to pass. Jesus was been recognized as the great person he is. He was being praised and honored by thousands of those in Jerusalem for the Passover, and I do mean thousands.

10 There were so many people that he didn't see us among the crowd. We certainly saw him. And I was not entirely pleased with what I saw. Jesus was not on a big white horse. He was on the colt of a donkey. A donkey! I couldn't believe my eyes. Surely he realized how ridiculous this looked for a King. 11 He just sat there looking very somber. I felt he looked really sad. On the other hand, Peter, who was walking beside him, was having a great time. He was waving at the crowd, smiling, and looking like he was really enjoying it all. 12 One thing which pleased me was that Jesus was wearing the beautiful tunic I had made for him. It really looked nice.

13 Later when some of our friends were discussing the excitement of the day, one of them mentioned he was surprised when Jesus began to sob. I sure couldn't figure out why he would be crying with all the triumphant joy surrounding him. Later I realized he was weeping because Jerusalem, the city of God, was rejecting the message of God's love and help being proclaimed by His Son. 14 I tried to put the donkey situation aside and to rejoice with the enormous crowd and their enthusiasm for Jesus. 15 It took me awhile to get to sleep that night, but I slept better than I had for a long time. 16 My first thoughts upon awakening the next day were again how I wished Joseph could have lived to see the multitudes giving honor to Jesus. He would have been so proud. 17 My mind went back over the many times Joseph and I had talked about how few people really

grasped who Jesus was and what he would be doing for Israel. We would talk about how the angel appeared to me privately. 18 I know Elizabeth sensed the presence of spiritual power when I entered their home as baby John leaped in her womb. 19 The shepherds knew a special child had entered the world because of the angels. It was because of a special star the Magi knew the King of Israel had arrived. 20 Simeon and Anna beheld the hand of God on him. We marveled as to how much through the years, that other than by these few, he was ignored, even by his brothers and sisters. I was so happy and thrilled that at last it seemed as though all Jerusalem had accepted him. I was really excited as I got into the day.

21 But my excitement was short lived. The next afternoon, John came to see me. After greeting me, he said, "Mary, did you hear what Jesus did when he got into the city?" 22 "No, what did he do?" was my response. John said, "Well, after the big parade, he went into the Temple. This time, he did not go there to pray, that is for sure. In fact, he became angry. Peter and I were right there with him and expected him to say something to persuade and convince the religious leaders to accept him and his teachings. 23 I still have a hard time understanding why he did it." "Well, out with it John," I blurted. "What did he do?" 24 "Mary, he took out a whip. I had never seen him have one of those before. I certainly never thought he would use it. But he did, I tell you, he did. He angrily dashed through the Court of the Gentiles, knocking over the tables of the money changers. 25 He opened the bird cages and released the birds. It was then he screamed, 'This Temple is my Father's house. It should be a house of prayer and you have made it a den of thieves!' 26 Then to make matters worse, the common folk loved what he was doing. They dashed into the Court of the Gentiles. The children

were loudly shouting praises to God. The Temple leaders were frantic. 27 They tried to shut up the children, but they yelled all the louder. The Temple leaders even tried to get Jesus to quiet them. Instead of quieting them, Jesus encouraged them to become even more excited. He said to the leaders that his Father could even make the stones cry out for joy."

28 All the time John is telling me this I am thinking, my Jesus, my Jesus, why did you do these ridiculous things? You had Israel in the palm of your hand and your foolish actions have undone all the good you have done. 29 John then said there was more. I said, "How can there be anything worse than this?" John said, "Mary, the lame, the blind, and the crippled began to crowd into the Temple area. When Jesus saw them, he welcomed them and healed them. 30 This activity climaxed it for the Temple priests. They were furious. I don't know what they will ultimately do, but believe me, it won't be good for Jesus, or for us, his disciples. Mary, I am scared, but I am still going to stick with Jesus. I love him and I know he loves and trusts me." 31 Neither myself, nor the girls, had a chance to talk with Jesus after these incidents. He kept busy preaching, teaching, and healing people. I was hoping he would join me and his sisters for the Passover dinner, but he didn't.

32 John came by to see me the next morning. It was evident he was upset about something. He greeted me and asked how I rested and other small talk. I finally said to him, "John, you are not yourself. What's wrong? Has something happened to Jesus?" 33 My questions opened the dam about what was bothering John. He nervously said, "Mary, Jesus has been arrested. He has been taken by the religious fanatics." "John what do you mean? Is he being accused of something? Is his life in danger?" 34 I continued with questions before John could answer any of them. "Was

he able to observe the Passover meal last night? I thought he would celebrate it at Mary and Martha's house with us, which he has done for the past several years. I was so disappointed he didn't come, and have wondered all night if he did observe it, and where and with whom?"

35 "Yes, Mary, he did observe the Passover supper. It was with us twelve disciples. And to be honest with you, I somewhat wish he had been with you and your friends. The meal was not as other such meals have been." "What do you mean, not as other Passover meals?" I asked. 36 "Mary," John said, "Let me tell you of the entire evening. It was a nightmare to me. I have never had such inner turmoil in my life."

37 I will never, ever forget my conversation with John concerning the events surrounding the last Passover meal Jesus celebrated with his disciples. I specifically asked him to fill me in on all the details of the night. 38 John then began to share his heart with me. "Mary, we could not understand why he was so subdued in spirit. He was so very different from the outgoing and positive Jesus we have known for over three years. There was no joy at this meal. 39 A couple of days ago he mentioned how eager he was to eat the Passover Meal with us. Some of his comments during the meal have us all puzzled. For instance, he took bread and broke it. Then he said 'This is my body which is broken for you. All of you eat of it. This do in remembrance of me.' 40 That was strange to us. He was with us, what is this remembrance business? We have no idea. And why wouldn't all of us eat of it, if he handed a piece to us. I can't figure it out. But it gets stranger.

41 "Near the end of the meal, he held a cup of wine and said, 'This is the new testament in my blood, which is shed for you. All of you drink of it.' Mary, now what is that all about? My blood shed for you? All of you drink of it?

42 Then he gave the cup first to me and motioned for me to
pass it around to all the others. We just didn't get it." 43 My
response was, "John, do you feel he is really beginning to
be afraid of the religious leaders? I don't know for sure, but
what you just told me leads me to think he feels he may
even be killed. God deliver us from such a calamity. But,
John, even though the bread and the cup incident puzzles
you, why are you so cast down, and you say the other
disciples are in the same mood?"

44 "Mary," he replied, "the big reason for all the
disciples being so down is during the meal Jesus abruptly
announced that one of us was going to betray him. Yes, we
were all appalled when Jesus, with deep emotion and tears
in his eyes, said that one of us in the room would betray
him. This really upset all of us. 45 A few immediately asked
him which one it would be. Others cried out in denial, 'Not
me!' Some also asked when it would be done. 46 As you can
well imagine, this deeply troubled all of us throughout the
whole evening. It seemed too crazy to publicly accuse one
of us twelve of betraying him, and especially to do this at
the Passover meal. It just didn't make sense to us. 47 Then
we became suspicious of each other. Yet, we didn't think
any one of us would ever betray him. Every one of us has
really being devoted to him and his teaching for nearly
three years. 48 Truly we really felt Jesus was more troubled
than he should be, especially after such a triumphant entry
into Jerusalem just a few days ago. Have not the crowds
wholeheartedly embraced him for the past several days?
49 And after all, to whom would he be betrayed, and why?
These were the thoughts which crossed our minds. 49 We
were confident that because of his huge following, the
religious leaders could not really do him any great harm,
and there would be no one else wanting to do away with
him. 50 So at the dinner, this betrayal business, although we

felt it to be very scary, we felt it was not possible. We dismissed it as something that would never happen."

51 By this time, I was really getting upset. Frustrated, I said to him, "John, what finally happened? You are giving me all these details, but what happened?" 52 After a long pause, he said, "Mary, later that evening, he was betrayed." "No!" I screamed. "But by whom?" In a hushed tone, John said, "By Judas." I couldn't help myself when through my tears I said, "But, John, why Judas? My dear Jesus trusted him so much. He even kept your money pouch. Why, oh why, would he do this?" 53 John hesitantly told me more startling news. He said, "You are going to find this hard to believe, but three times during the night, Peter denied he even knew Jesus, let alone that he was one of his disciples."

54 I couldn't believe my ears were hearing that Peter denied the Master. I asked John, "Where is Peter now?" "Mary, I have no idea where he is, or even could be. The last time I saw him he was sobbing and crying like a parent who had just lost a child by death. 55 I truly have no idea where he ended up or where he is at the moment. And I am really concerned about Judas and where he is and what he is doing. I can't see how he will be able to live with himself after his dastardly deed of betraying Jesus. God help him."

56 After I had shed a lot of tears and got settled somewhat, I asked John to tell me further details surrounding the supper and the rest of the evening. The following is, to the best of my memory, what he told me. It was not pleasant, but at least I got the truth. It hurt, but I am glad he told me what really happened. 57 Even as I tell this to you these many years later, I can't get Peter out of my mind. I want to assure you that Jesus continued to love him. In fact, after his resurrection, Jesus told the women to personally tell Peter he was alive and would be meeting with him. Jesus certainly forgave Peter. 58 And really, I honestly

believe Jesus would have forgiven Judas, if he had not hung himself from a tree. Can you believe he betrayed Jesus for only thirty pieces of silver? Why, that is the price of a lowly slave. It is unbelievable Judas would stoop that low.

59 Joses, I have gotten sidetracked. I must get back to the night of the betrayal and arrest of Jesus. Here are more of the details of the night as John gave them to me. 60 He said, "Even when Judas left early, we didn't associate betrayal with his leaving. We just thought it might be to get something that Jesus felt he needed at the moment, or to give some money to the poor. After all, he kept the money pouch and often purchased items, as well as frequently gave money to the poor." 61 "When did he return?" I asked. John said, "That was the mystery to us, Mary. He didn't return. The meal ended and we sang a hymn and headed for our customary place in the Garden of Gethsemane. We naturally thought Judas would catch up with us, or at least he knew where we would be when he finally decided to rejoin us. We often went to the same place in the garden.

62 "Arriving in the garden without Judas, Jesus pointed out a spot for the eleven of us to sit and rest for awhile. He said he wanted to spend some time alone in prayer with the Father. 63 Then he said, 'Peter, James, and John, come with me.' We went a short distance further and he told us to rest and to be in prayer. He went about a stone's throw from the three of us to pray. We had never heard him pray so fervently and so loud. 64 I will never forget his words, 'Father, if it be possible, let this cup pass from me, but nevertheless not my will, but thine be done'."

65 "How long did he pray?" I asked. John replied, "It must have been for at least an hour. The three of us chatted for several minutes after Jesus had gone to pray. 66 We still couldn't figure out why Judas had not arrived. James said he hoped he had not been robbed, wounded, or even killed.

Peter lamented that Judas had not stayed with our group. 67 He pointed out how he would have been safe with the group. Peter said the big reason he always carried a sword was to let any tempted robbers know they would be in grave danger if they tried to rob the disciples. 68 He truly believed his sword was a silent witness that we are willing and able to protect ourselves. Judas especially needed protection as he carried the money pouch. 69 Peter truly believed a visible sword is good preventive procedure. He felt when would-be robbers saw his sword they would assume each of the other disciples were probably carrying one, or at least has a knife hidden under his tunic. 70 There is no doubt Peter felt being armed is a deterrent to being robbed or killed, even though Jesus taught that he who lives by the sword dies by the sword. 71 Yet, he never did tell Peter not to carry a sword. James mentioned he was glad to hear Simon say he also had a sword with him. He pointed out how Simon was an expert with a sword. He had resisted the Romans for years and had been in many dangerous fights with them."

72 For some reason, I was interested as to the disciples' response to Jesus saying to get a sword. John continued, "We discussed how surprised we were when during supper Jesus said to get a sword, and if necessary, sell a garment to get money to buy one. 73 When Peter and Simon the Zealot admitted having one with them, Jesus said that two swords would be enough. They sure didn't know what he was getting at, but were glad they had brought a sword with them. They both felt maybe Jesus was at last beginning to face the realities of street gangs and the necessity of being armed."

74 John related how all three of them were so tired and sleepy. He said, "The last thing I remember before falling asleep was James saying, 'I am really worried about Judas.

He should have been here by now. He knows where we always come to here in the garden. I hope no tragedy has befallen him.'" 75 My response to John was, "Yes, it is strange that Judas was gone for so long." John ignored my interruption and continued with the details of the night. 76 "I don't know exactly how long we were asleep. It must have been at least an hour. Jesus rather rudely awakened us in a tone of voice we had never heard him use before toward any of the disciples. 77 He woke us by sternly and loudly saying, 'What, could you not even stay awake one hour with me?' This cutting question really made the three of us feel terrible. 78 Then Jesus said, 'Get up! Let us be going, my hour is at hand.' At that moment we had no idea what he was talking about, but we soon found out."

79 "Why? What happened next?" I asked. "Mary, we had walked only a short way from where Jesus had been praying when we noticed torches coming up the hill. 80 We couldn't imagine who would be coming into the garden at this hour of the night. As they drew near, it was obvious there were as many as fifty men in the crowd. 81 What really surprised us was when the mob got near, Judas was with them. We couldn't believe it! What was he doing with this group of ruffians? Had they captured him and the money purse and had now come to try to get more from us? 82 Peter spoke up and said, 'Judas, what's wrong? What are they doing to you? Can we help you?' Judas never even looked at Peter, but hung his head for a moment. 83 He abruptly straightened up and went straight to Jesus, and kissed him on the cheek. It was then the leader stepped forward and said to Jesus, 'You are under arrest. Come with us.' 84 We were horrified! Now it hit us with full force. Judas! He was the betrayer! We all now realized the real reason he had left the dinner early and why he had not

joined us in the garden. He was betraying the Master! We couldn't believe it. It was frightening."

85 I asked, "What did you do? Didn't you try to save Jesus? Surely you could have gotten away from that mob." John said, "Yes, I immediately felt we should flee and hide in the garden. I knew they couldn't find us. 86 Peter must have been reading my mind, because he whispered to me, 'John, you grab Jesus and run and tell the other disciples to run with you when I attack this mob. I am going to attack the young man standing by the leader. 87 He won't be able to defend anyone when I get through with him. They will get distracted with me and my sword. You all can then run and hide. They will never be able to find you in the garden as dark as it is. Don't worry about me. I will catch up with you later.' 88 The next thing I knew, Peter had charged the young man and swung at him with his sword. I grabbed Jesus and shouted, "Let's get out of here!" Jesus strongly resisted my efforts to get him to join us and run away. Instead he sternly and loudly said, 'Peter, put away your sword. NOW! 89 The only blood to be shed is my own for the redemption of all who will believe in me. My Father told me I must drink the full cup of suffering. I am going to obey and honor Him.'

90 "There was no doubt he meant what he said, and said what he meant. The young man Peter had attacked was screaming with pain and blood was gushing from his ear. 91 Peter's surprise attack had left the mob in great confusion. The mob evidently felt we all had a sword, or at least a knife. At that moment, we could have very easily gotten away with Jesus."

92 I was so stunned and angry by John's words I practically shouted at him, "Why, oh why, didn't Jesus go with you? It seems foolish to me that he would just meekly let them take him away as a prisoner without putting up a

fight. 93 If he wasn't willing to resist, why didn't he ask the Father to send angels to protect him? John, this horrifying news is breaking my heart!"

94 "Well, Mary, let me tell you the rest of the details. All of a sudden things changed completely. Jesus said to the young man whose ear was hanging to the side of his head by a piece of skin, 'Come here.' 95 He took a few steps toward Jesus as Jesus moved towards him. For some reason at that moment everyone, the mob as well as us disciples, were standing as if we were statues unable to move. 96 It was then the miracle took place. Jesus reached out and touched the young man's ear. Right before our very eyes the ear was restored as before. The bleeding stopped. The pain was gone. 97 Momentarily we felt the victory had been won. The mob surely would not arrest Jesus after seeing this miracle. But to our amazement, after several seconds of stunned silence on our part, and the mob, the leader said to Jesus, 'You are under arrest. Come with us. The High Priest wants to talk with you tonight.' 98 That was the first hint we had as to whom was seeking his arrest. Jesus calmly asked, 'Why do you come here to arrest me? I have been in the city teaching all week long and you didn't arrest me.' The leader simply replied, 'What is that to you? Come, we must be going.' 99 With that, they melted into the darkness with Jesus. We were shocked, yes stunned, when Judas went with them. 100 We practically cried for Judas, and literally did for Jesus. We were absolutely dumbfounded that the one who had set so many free from sickness and despair was now a prisoner."

101 I have never known John to be as upset as he was when telling me about that dreadful night. Joses, as you know, this all took place many years ago. I must tell you that it was not until after Pentecost and the coming of the Holy Spirit that John and the other disciples realized what

Jesus meant when he told them of his death and resurrection. 102 They then remembered he had told them more than once of his death and resurrection. However, at those times, they were not able to comprehend what he was telling them. 103 They now knew the Father had revealed the future to Jesus, and that Jesus was not hesitant in any way, or at any time, to be obedient to his Father. He completely and joyfully accepted the Father's will for his life, death, and resurrection. He always believed. He always obeyed. He truly was without sin.

104 John went on to tell me, "Jesus was taken to the house of Caiaphas where evidently the Sanhedrin was in special session, expecting him to be brought before them. I don't know what went on in there, but we were told Jesus was put in prison for the night." 105 I was really disturbed by John's report. I asked, "How long will Jesus be in prison?" John didn't know for sure. He said he felt it wouldn't be too long. 106 He also said they would probably punish Jesus, warn him to quit his teaching, and then let him go on probation. I asked, "Do you think they might kill him?" 107 John said, "I feel, with the present popularity of Jesus, they wouldn't dare kill him." He went on to say they had no power to kill him. He reminded me the Romans had taken this power away from the Jews.

108 His answers comforted me some. However, I was still very worried and deeply concerned. 109 I thought to myself, why did Jesus do such foolish things in the sacred Temple? If he had not done such stupid things, he could have prevented all of this upheaval. He could have, he could have, yes, he could have, just kept flooding my mind. Oh God, he could have done things so differently.

Chapter 18

೭∞⊗

1 It was early afternoon before John reported to me again. He said, "The religious leaders accused Jesus of many things, but none of their accusations could be proven true. They even paid some unscrupulous men to bring false accusations against him. All of these efforts failed. 2 Then they took him to Pilate. After talking to Jesus, he couldn't discern where he had broken any laws. He quickly decided to let him go free. The leaders soundly rejected his decision. 3 So Pilate sent Jesus to Herod. Herod was glad to see him in person, but could find nothing of great consequence that Jesus had done wrong. So he sent him back to Pilate. 4 Pilate pressed the mob of Jews as to what he had done wrong. They then yelled out he had said he was the King of the Jews. They said to Pilate they had no King but Caesar. 5 This accusation seemed to affect Pilate more than anything else they had said. He sure didn't want news to get back to Caesar that he had let another King rise up among the people. 6 From what I hear, Pilate's wife warned him not to do anything against Jesus. She told him she had been warned in a dream Jesus was a righteous man, and Pilate should not give in to the shouting of the Jews for his death.

7 "Pilate told the mob he could find no fault in him. They had been crying out, 'Crucify him, crucify him,' but

Pilate couldn't believe they meant it. 8 It was evident he was really struggling to get out of this mess, and with saving his own skin, as well as saving Jesus. 9 He then tried one last desperate thing. He reminded them that each year at Passover time a prisoner was released. He proceeded to give them a choice. 10 He said, 'Do you want me to release Jesus or Barabbas?' Everyone knew Barabbas was the most notorious prisoner held by the Romans here in Jerusalem. 11 Pilate evidently felt there would be no doubt they, in all fairness, would want Jesus released. To his amazement they shouted to release Barabbas. He then had Jesus stand before them. He bluntly asked them, 'What shall I do with this man?' 12 He was shocked with the venom of the angry mob as they loudly shouted, 'Crucify him, crucify him!' He again said, 'But why, what harm has he done?' His words fell on deaf ears. They only shouted all the louder, 'We have no King, but Caesar. Crucify him, Crucify him, *Crucify him!!*'

13 "Pilate had a servant bring him a bowl of water. He washed his hands saying, 'I want to cleanse my hands of this whole matter. This man is innocent.' 14 In their fury they shouted back to let his blood be on their hands. They insisted he should be crucified. Pilate then commanded his men to carry out his order to have Jesus crucified. 15 The crucifixion of two thieves was already scheduled for this afternoon, so they can crucify Jesus at the same time. 16 Jesus received no mercy from the soldiers. They took him into one of the halls, removed his clothes and put a purple robe on him. Some of them mockingly said, 'Hail, King of the Jews!' 17 One of them broke off some thorn bush branches and quickly wove them into a crude crown. He forcefully pushed it on the head of Jesus. 18 Immediately blood began to flow. They continued to mock him saying, 'Hail, King of the Jews.'" 19 At this point of John's report I

was getting sick to my stomach. It was unimaginable that men would do this to a wonderful and kind man as Jesus. 20 'King of the Jews' flashed through my mind. What I pictured sure didn't fit this situation. John went on to tell me. "Finally tired of harassing Jesus, they removed the robe and had him put on his clothes. 21 They were now heading toward the Hill of the Skull. They had already come up with a heavy cross for Jesus. The crosses for the two criminals were evidently already at the crucifixion site. 22 Two of the soldiers started to carry it. They hadn't gone far until they put it down. They looked sternly at Jesus and ordered him, 'Pick it up. You carry it. We are not going to tire ourselves out.' 23 Obediently he accepted the burden of the cross. It was obvious it is very heavy. He at times stumbled under its weight. Finally, he just couldn't go on any further. He was very near total exhaustion. 24 It was then the soldiers spotted a big strong man in the crowd of those lining the street to witness this tragedy. They commanded him to carry the cross. They will soon be to Golgotha, but I wanted to come tell you what was going on."

25 I couldn't take any more. I cried out that I wanted to go down and see Jesus. John tried to talk me out of going, but I frantically insisted. 26 The two of us hurried to Golgotha and found a spot nearby the Hill of the Skull. It was where we could easily see what was taking place. 27 Sure enough, shortly after we got to this place where we could have a good view of the hill, the soldiers in charge of Jesus came into sight. 28 It was as John had told me. Someone else was carrying the cross. We learned later it was Simon of Cyrene who was forced to do this. 29 Jesus was struggling just to walk. I wanted to cover my eyes and wipe it all out of my mind, but I couldn't. I had to see my son, even though he was now being treated as a common

criminal. 30 I admit there were times I felt, if he continued preaching as he did, he might be stoned to death. But it had never entered my mind he might someday be crucified. What a painful, horrible, humiliating, way to die.

31 I must confess, with all which had happened the last few days and his entering the city triumphantly, I really felt they wouldn't kill him. Plus, I knew the strict law of the Romans prohibited Jews from putting anyone to death. 32 But the religious leaders had devised an evil scheme to accomplish their goal by using the Romans. Clever, I thought, but oh so very cruel. 33 As they got closer I clung even tighter to John. They took their good old time. I guess it was to give the people a view of what horrible fate awaits anyone defying Rome. There were a large number witnessing this horrible crucifixion. But it was very small compared to the crowd from just a few days before who had welcomed him into the city. 34 They finally arrived and started to ascend the hill. We could see the other two crosses. A few minutes later, soldiers brought the two criminal prisoners. 35 Shortly afterwards, the soldiers arrived with Jesus. We hardly recognized him. It was obvious he had been beaten. Blood had clotted on his face. His hair was all matted with blood. 36 My heart went out to him. I wanted to dash out and comfort him. John constrained me. But believe me, it was so hard for me to keep from trying to get to Jesus. 37 The criminals did not go to the cross meekly. One of them fiercely fought being put on the cross. It was a struggle, yet the four Roman soldiers finally got him there. They held down his arms while the nails were driven in. It was horrible. 38 The sound of the hammer hitting the nail filled the air with evil. I wondered how the soldiers could even participate in such a torturous act. But you know, they looked as though they actually enjoyed it. I couldn't believe my eyes. 39 It was now Jesus

to whom they turned their full attention. They took off his clothes and laid them aside for the moment. 40 Then they did something different from what had been done for the other two. They nailed a board near the top of the cross. It looked like there was writing on it. We could not make out the words. 41 Jesus humbly, and without a trace of fear, went to the cross. He offered no resistance. On his own, he laid down on the cross. This seemed to surprise the soldiers. He held out both arms for the nails to be driven into the palms of his hands. 42 I shrieked at the first blow of the hammer, and every blow after that, as the nails were one by one hammered into his hands and feet. My heart almost burst in agony. 43 Finally this ordeal was finished. They raised the cross and dropped it in the hole. I screamed, "No, No, NO" at the top of my lungs. Through my gushing tears, I could now set my eyes on what I had so longed to see: ***This is Jesus, the King of the Jews.*** I nearly fainted with grief. Yes, they were the right words, but were appearing on a cross of death, and not above a throne of life and power.

44 I felt I could not go on living. Jesus was acknowledged as King of the Jews, but by whom? By the evil Romans! Most certainly the religious leaders would never say this especially now at the time of his death.

Chapter 19

❧

1 We later found out that those who sought to have Jesus crucified also tried to get Pilate to not put the sign on the cross. However, he would not listen to them. He just sternly told them, "That which I have written, I have written." 2 I couldn't get that sight out of my mind. Yes, the Magi had called him the King of the Jews. Surely they could not have conceived that he would receive such a title at the time he was killed by being nailed to a cross. 3 I cried out, "Angel, where are you now? You told me he would be born. Now, please come and tell me he will not die. Please, come and rescue him." 4 John kept saying to me, "Mary, I am so sorry, please try to control yourself, I am so sorry you must watch this. Just try to think of all the good Jesus has done." These words pierced my heart. 5 In bitter anger, I said, "John, it is simply because of all the good he has done that I think God has betrayed both him and me by letting him die on that cross. Can't you see? He is not dying a natural death! He is being crucified on a cross between two common criminals. I just can't understand it. 6 I will never forgive you and his other disciples for forsaking him. Why didn't you all do something? You all could have used a sword like Peter did, and then, along with Jesus, escaped from them." 7 John felt terrible, and keep saying, "Please, Mary, please." I couldn't figure out the significance of all

this 'please' business. My life was ending on this day. Jesus was being crucified and I was slowly dying a death of sorrow. 8 I went on to say, "I will never forgive you or the religious leaders. I blame you and the disciples and the religious leaders even more than I do the Romans. And I will never be able to forgive any of you."

9 Our conversation along those lines ended as we noticed the soldiers were dividing the garments of Jesus among themselves. 10 They got to the tunic I had made for him. It was one large piece of cloth. They were about to rip it into four equal pieces. I cried out, "No. Don't do that! Please!!" John quickly got me to be quiet. He said, "Mary, if you cause a disturbance, you will end up in trouble. They will do what they want to do. You are not going to stop them." 11 We saw it was evident they did not want to ruin the tunic. They decided to cast lots for it. The one who won the tunic was elated. I thought, how horrible can it become? The tunic I felt to be fit for a King was now in the possession of a Roman soldier. 12 He would have no idea of the love which had gone into it, the reason for it being made, or that it was made by his mother. I nearly fainted with grief.

13 It was at this time Jesus spoke. I marveled he had the strength to utter a word. I marveled even more at what he spoke. It was, *"Father, forgive them for they know not what they do."* 14 Forgive them? How could the Father forgive anyone for killing the one who was to deliver his people? It didn't make sense. 15 I said, "John, did you hear him?" He said, "Of course I did, Mary." "But John, do you really think the Father should forgive them?" John's response was, "Mary, knowing what Jesus taught, I would have to say he means it when he asks the Father for them to be forgiven. I learned long ago Jesus always said what he meant, and meant what he said. And yes, Mary, I believe the Father will grant the request of Jesus. He truly will

forgive them, if they turn to Him and sincerely seek forgiveness." 16 Before we could go on with that topic, the one criminal started frantically screaming and cursing at Jesus. He challenged him to get himself and them down from the cross, if he was really the Son of God. 17 Jesus didn't respond. A few moments later the other criminal chastised the one who had spoken so rudely to Jesus. He said, "We deserve our punishment. This man has done nothing wrong, and yet he is being killed." 18 Then he said to Jesus, "Lord, remember me when you come into your kingdom." 19 My racing mind thought, "What kingdom?" Kingdom was out of the picture now. The only thing left was death and a grave. 20 But Jesus turned to this thief and said what to me was one of the most baffling things I have ever heard. He said, *"This day you shall be with me in paradise."* I thought, "Jesus, how do you think you are going to go from a cross to paradise? And to go there today? You are crazy!" 21 Jesus must have perceived my agony, and with a tender voice said, *"John, behold your mother, and Mary, behold your son."* 22 It was then my breaking heart almost melted. This was the Jesus I knew. He was always loving, kind, and compassionate. He truly had a love and concern for others. I held to John tighter than ever. Little did I realize how much I would need John, and how much John would need me.

23 Then a frightening thing began to happen. A very dark cloud arose in the east. It began to rapidly spread across the sky. The sky started to become ominous and gloomy. It wasn't long until the darkness was deeper than the darkest night I had ever experienced. 24 This darkness lasted for three hours. Many of the people began to leave when the darkness started to engulf us. They were frightened and wanted to get away from the agony and horribleness of this crucifixion. 25 About two hours into this

dark period, there was a powerful earthquake. It was very scary. 26 Throughout the time, we had not been able to see the men on the crosses. We thought they had all died for we heard no sound from them. 27 Then, as the darkness began to fade, we heard Jesus cry with a loud voice: "*My God, my God, why have you forsaken me?*" 28 As the light began to conquer the darkness, we were able to perceive Jesus was more gaunt than ever and barely alive. 29 His cry of being forsaken by God struck a sensitive cord in my heart. I was thinking the same thing about myself. At this very moment, I was feeling terrible and abandoned by God. 30 Would you believe, when Jesus said he felt forsaken by God, I felt a little better? If this good and just man could feel abandoned by God, I certainly had a right to feel the same. Or at least that is what I told myself. 31 A few minutes later, Jesus said, "*I thirst.*" One of the soldiers put a sponge soaked in sour wine to his lips. He refused it. 32 It was now after three in the afternoon. Jesus struggled to muster enough strength to say, "*Father, into thy hands I commend my spirit.*" 33 Almost immediately afterwards, in a remarkably loud voice he cried out, "***It is finished!***" His head fell and his whole body shuddered. It was obvious he had died. He was gone, and in my heart I felt disparately alone. 34 My being the mother of a King was not to be. Jesus as King of the Jews and as our deliverer was an illusion. It was all over.

35 Years later John and I were discussing when Jesus died and how terrible it was. It was then John pointed out to me that it was interesting Jesus died at the approximate time the Temple priests were killing the Passover lamb. 36 He told me a lot of people were now saying the timing fit what John the Baptist had proclaimed, that "Jesus was the Lamb of God who takes away the sin of the world."

37 After Jesus was buried, John persuaded me to leave. He took me to my room where the girls were worried

almost sick over my having been gone so long. They were beginning to think that perhaps some tragedy had befallen me. 38 As you can well imagine, I got very little sleep that night. The next day I didn't know what to do, but to stay in my room. John stopped to see me in the afternoon.

39 He told me two very interesting things. First, that some who were aware of the moment when Jesus died, and also knew when the veil of the Temple was torn in two, said these things happened at the same time. 40 He then told me something I did not know, he said the 60 by 20 foot veil is as thick as the palm of his hand. A team of horses would not be able to pull it apart. Further, the tear started at the top and came down. No human could have torn it, especially that way. It had to be an act of God. The death of Jesus had now made possible direct access to the Father. 41 The Holy of Holies was not really an earthly place protected by a veil. The reality, as it was now revealed, is that it is in heaven and it is open to all believers. Anyone who believes can now approach the Father with boldness.

42 The next thing John told me was almost unbelievable. He said that during the earthquake, some of the graves outside of Jerusalem gave up their dead. There were individuals who came out of those graves, and people who had known them in life, saw them again. This was a miracle no one could have imagined. It certainly was hard to believe.

43 I want to give you some details of the burial of Jesus. John and I stayed until he was buried. We knew this would be done before sunset, because it would then be the Sabbath. 44 The crowds had left, as well as the soldiers. The three on the crosses were left alone. A couple of hours before sunset, four soldiers came back to check the crucified ones. They broke the legs of the thieves. This needless act was sickening. 45 They came to Jesus and saw

he was already dead and so they didn't break any of his bones. One of the soldiers did a seemingly senseless thing. He plunged a spear into the side of Jesus. Blood and water gushed forth. It was very gruesome. 46 I got sick to my stomach and again began to cry uncontrollably. John's presence was a comfort to me and got me through this almost unbearable experience. How I wished you boys could have been with me. It would have been a comfort to me. Later I was grateful you never witnessed this horrible experience, since you didn't arrive until the day of the Passover.

47 We had no idea where they would bury the thieves. We thought it would probably be Potter's Field, where the indigent were buried. 48 We wondered what they would do with the body of Jesus. Then we saw two men approaching the crosses. I recognized the one man as Joseph of Arimathaea. He was very rich and a prominent leader in Jerusalem. 49 I didn't recognize the other man, but John did. He said the man's name was Nicodemus. He went on to say he was one of the religious leaders. 50 He said Jesus had told him that Nicodemus had secretly met with him one night, as he was very interested in spiritual things. However, he was also very fearful as to what would happen to his career if others found out he talked to Jesus. 51 Jesus shared with John he told Nicodemus of God's love for the world and that all should believe in His son. Jesus told him, as he had more than once told the disciples, that to understand spiritual things you must be born again.

52 We watched as they respectfully cared for the body of Jesus. We then followed them to where he was buried. It was in a nearby garden. 53 I was so touched that a rich man buried Jesus in his own personal tomb. Although it was awful he had died an ugly death by crucifixion, it was of some comfort to know his body ended up in a beautiful garden.

54 I am sure you recall that you and your brothers returned home the day after Passover. You were all stunned and grief stricken over the death of Jesus. It wasn't until several days later you heard of the resurrection. 55 Of course, you didn't really believe he was alive until after I got home. Your believing started after I told you of my visit with him in the garden, and that the women and others had seen him.

56 I want to tell you I really couldn't sleep the night of the crucifixion. In the wee hours of the morning I thought of how he started his life with us by being born in a lowly stable. It had ended with him being buried in a borrowed tomb. 57 And then the awful thought hit me, John's birth was announced by an angel. The birth of Jesus was announced by an angel. Yet, both men ended up being killed by evil men. This sure did not make any sense to me. 58 In my anguish, I cried out to God for his comfort. I also told him I felt that so often life just isn't fair. In fact, I went even further and told Him sometimes it is, without a doubt, a very, very cruel experience.

Chapter 20

❧❧

1 The beauty of the garden could not hide the hideousness of his brutal death. In no way could it remove the pain of grief consuming my entire being. 2 He had lived a life of constantly helping others. Yet, his life ended with him having nothing, and receiving help from no one, even God. It didn't make any sense to me. 3 Within a day, the rumor was being spread Jesus would be raised from the dead after three days. I must admit I had disturbing doubts about the truthfulness of this ridiculous rumor. 4 My logic was that Jesus was the one who raised the dead. Now he was dead, so who was going to raise him? No, I just knew this was the end. But Joses, I can now say it really wasn't. In reality, it was just the beginning of even more amazing revelations of the love and power of God. 5 We heard the religious leaders had asked Pilate to have soldiers guard the tomb for at least three days. 6 They told him Jesus had said he would be killed, but in three days rise again. They said they didn't believe him, but were concerned his disciples might come and steal the body and then tell people he had risen from the dead. Pilate consented and soldiers were at the tomb the very next day after he was buried.

7 John came back the next day to check on me. I had slept very little and was near total exhaustion. I was overwhelmed with grief, and totally exhausted physically and

emotionally. 8 My women friends were finding it equally difficult to cope with all that happened to Jesus. Some of them had often traveled with Jesus. They were of great help to him and the disciples. They were very close to him and loved his ministry.

9 A few of us decided we would go to the tomb early in morning on the third day. It was not that we really believed Jesus would be raised from the dead. For some reason, we just wanted to be there. 10 We didn't fear going into the garden as we knew soldiers would be guarding the tomb and no harm would befall us. When we got to the place where we could see the garden area, we were surprised. We didn't see any soldiers. Where had they gone? We had no idea. 11 It was getting fully daylight as we neared the tomb. As it came into full view, we were stopped in our tracks. Our mouths opened in wide amazement. 12 Almost in unison we proclaimed, "It is open!" We couldn't believe it. Who rolled the stone away? What is going on? It still had not hit us that he may be alive. A resurrection miracle never entered our minds. This thought was too unreal for it to be a part of our conscious thinking. 13 We cautiously, and some-what timidly, approached the open tomb. There was no doubt somebody, somehow, had rolled the stone away. Had the disciples actually gotten away with stealing his body? 14 This was the prominent thought which crossed our minds. But how could they have done it with the soldiers guarding the tomb? And where were the soldiers? Our minds were in a whirl.

15 We all jumped to the same logical conclusion. We just knew somebody had stolen his body. Mary Magdalene didn't hesitate. She dashed to tell Peter and John someone had taken the body of Jesus. She told them we had no idea where they had taken it. 16 The two men ran to check it out. John was the first to arrive. He just looked into the tomb.

Peter arrived and immediately ran into the tomb. It was obvious Jesus was gone, but they still did not believe he had risen from the dead. Such a glorious thought did not cross their mind. They didn't tarry long.

17 Prior to their coming, I had gone some distance from the tomb and sat on a rock and wept. Sometime later, a man approached me and said, "Why are you weeping?" 18 I said, "Because they have taken the body of my son, Jesus. Do you know where they have taken it?" His reply was simply, "Mary." 19 With that, I knew it was Jesus. I shrieked, "My dear son, Jesus," and started to embrace him. 20 He gently stopped me, and said. "No, Mary, God's son." He went on to say, "Please do not touch me, as I have not yet ascended to my Father." 21 At the time, I didn't understand what this all meant. Further, I was really taken back because this was the first time he had ever called me Mary. It flashed through my mind, why didn't he say, Mother? 22 Later in the day the truth dawned upon me. It became clear he was now to be seen as the Son of God, not as my son. He was no longer to be earthly, but heavenly. This made sense to me and settled my spirit.

23 I must get back to the garden and my encounter with Jesus. I almost felt like I was dreaming. I had a chance to talk with him for only a few minutes. 24 He went on to say, "Mary, when I completely emptied myself of my glories and power, I came to earth as any other baby enters the world. 25 The Father has told me that soon He will be returning me to all of my former glory and power and more. He will now also give me all the redeemed. 26 Mary, I know you had hoped I would become King of the Jews. I could have been Israel's King. I could have asked the Father for deliverance and He would have sent thousands of angels to help me. Neither Jew nor Gentile could have stood in their presence. 27 However, this would not have

accomplished the purpose of my coming into the world. I want to assure you, I will be King, not just of the Jews, but of all peoples, in all nations, and of all ages. And not for just a few fleeting years, but for all eternity. 28 Mary, I will be back for you and all others who have, and who will, believe in me. I came as man in a lowly stable. I will come again, yet the next time it will be in the sky as the Son of God, riding, not on a colt of a donkey, but on a great white horse. 29 I will carry a banner to be seen by all which will say: "King of Kings and Lord of Lords!" At that time I will answer to no man, but all men will answer to me and my Father. 30 It is then when every knee shall bow before me. The Father will then give all things into my hands. Mary, do not fret for I will be with you always." 31 He told me to go with the other women to tell the disciples he was alive, and he would be meeting with them soon. He then disappeared.

32 I must tell you, it never crossed my mind this short visit in the garden would be the last time I would see him. In my mind, I was visualizing Jesus being even more popular than Lazarus. So you can appreciate how impossible it is for me to really convey to you how thrilled I was to see him. Jesus was alive! Now, the whole world would truly be following him. 33 I was walking on cloud nine. I was so happy. The horribleness of the crucifixion was behind me. The glories of Jesus ultimately being King of the Jews really consumed me. Huge crowds had come out to see Lazarus after he came back from the grave. Now, Jesus is back. He and Lazarus will make the perfect team to get the whole world to honor them. 34 Only two individuals had ever spent a few days dead in a tomb, and come back to life. And to think I knew both of them. One was my son, and one was my son's good friend. Wow! 35 I felt it would be just a matter of time until I would see him again.

Everything was falling into place. Jesus appeared heavenly handsome. He would be looked upon as the greatest man of all time. At last, I would truly be the mother of the King. 36 I thought to myself, "Just wait until I tell his sisters and brothers. At last, our family is famous. No more stables or humble homes. The riches of this world are now within our family's reach."

37 At that time I sure wasn't concerned about the next world. I had it all right here, or so I thought. No one, absolutely no one, had ever experienced what had happened to my precious son. He came back from the grave. He was alive and well. My mind and heart were exploding with joy.

38 I was still in this state of shock and joy when Mary Magdalene came over to where I was standing and rejoicing in knowing Jesus was alive. She told me how she saw two angels. They asked her why she was weeping. 39 She told them they had taken her Lord and she knew not where they had taken him. She was frightened and still crying. 40 She said as she turned around, she saw a man she thought was the gardener. He asked her the same thing he asked me. "Why are you weeping?" 41 She said to him, "They have taken away my Lord, and I don't know where they have taken him. If you know, please tell me where they have taken him." 42 This man then said to her, "Mary." It was then she knew it was Jesus. She said she cried out, "Master!" Jesus spoke to her as he did to me. He said, "Please, don't touch me as I have not yet ascended to my Father."

43 As you can imagine, we were one excited group of ladies as we hurried back to tell the disciples. They didn't say they didn't believe us, but it was obvious they thought we had lost it. 44 Peter later told John an interesting thing he noticed in the tomb. It was about the cloth which had been

around the head of Jesus. It was the way it was folded. 45 As you know, one of our customs is that if you are a guest at a home for dinner, or a banquet, and do not like the food you fold your napkin a special way. You don't say anything to the host, but the way the napkin is folded speaks volumes. It tells the host you did not like the dinner. 46 Peter told John the head piece was folded in the same way. It was as though Jesus was saying, "I don't like the taste of death." At least it appears this was the message he was seeking to impart.

47 I have no idea as to how many times he appeared to others after his resurrection. John has told me about some of them. Sad to say, I never saw him again after my time in the garden with him. I thought I would see him often, and learn much, but it was not to be. John has told me about a few times he appeared to individuals and groups. 48 He never did appear to as huge of a crowd as the one which greeted him when he entered Jerusalem. John said he heard Jesus appeared to a crowd of about five hundred making it the largest group anyone remembers seeing him at after his resurrection.

49 John told me the first time he appeared to the disciples they were in a locked room. John related these details. He said, "It was the evening of the same day we went to the tomb. 50 Suddenly, Jesus was in the room with us. We had no idea how he entered the room. 51 I absolutely know the door was securely locked. Jesus spoke to us rather sternly about our unbelief. He then breathed upon us and said, 'Receive the Holy Spirit.' At the time, we had no idea what this was all about. One thing we did know for sure was Jesus was alive and well and had been in the room. 52 Thomas wasn't with us. When he showed up, we excitedly told him Jesus was alive. True to form, Thomas didn't believe us. He said he would not believe until he had

seen the nail marks, and the scar where the spear entered the body of Jesus."

53 John went on to say, "About eight days later, we were together again and Thomas was with us. Of course, we had the door securely locked. We were still very fearful of what might happen to us. 54 Miraculously, Jesus appeared in our midst. It was obvious Thomas didn't know what to say. Jesus broke the silence with, 'Thomas, behold my hands. And put your hand on the scar where the spear entered.'" 55 Then John said, "You should have seen the look on Thomas' face. He never touched Jesus. He immediately fell to his knees and blurted out 'My Lord and my God.' 56 Jesus told him to stand up. He then said to him. 'It is good, Thomas, you have seen and believed. But more blessed are those who have not seen and yet have believed.' 57 We wondered then as to whom he was talking about. Who were those who would believe even though they had never seen? We hadn't yet grasped the fact that his message of God's love and willingness to help would quickly spread to many nations."

58 John also told me two men came to the disciples and told them that while they were walking from Jerusalem to Emmaus, they unexpectedly encountered Jesus. 59 This is how it happened. They told the disciples a man joined them on their walk. He asked them why they looked so sad. 60 They responded they were surprised he was from the area and had not heard about Jesus being killed. They then said this stranger began to relate how Moses and the prophets had spoken about such a person. He pointed out to them many of the prophecies which had been made about Jesus, and how they had come to pass. 61 They invited him to have dinner. He said a prayer of thanks for the food. Then all of a sudden, he was gone. 62 It was then they realized he was Jesus, the risen one. Needless to say, they

didn't finish their meal. They were too excited to keep eating. They hurried back to tell the disciples they had actually seen Jesus. 63 They acknowledged to each other, after Jesus left them, that during the time he was talking with them they had a strange feeling of peace and glory come over them.

64 There is one more incident that really affected John. He said, "Several days had passed and there had been no further appearances to us by Jesus. 65 One day Peter announced he was going fishing. A number of us decided to go with him. We fished all night but did not catch a single fish. We were tired and disappointed as we headed toward the shore. 66 We were still quite a ways out in the water, when we noticed there was a man standing on the shore. He evidently was cooking something, because we saw smoke drifting into the air. 67 He yelled at us and asked if we had caught any fish. We told him no. We marveled at how we could hear him so well, even though we were still a long way from shore. 68 He said, 'Cast your net on the other side.' We had already given up on casting anywhere and we wondered what difference would it make which side of the boat we cast the net. 69 I can't tell you exactly what made us do it, but even though we were bone-tired, we unfurled the net and cast it on the other side. Lo and behold, almost immediately, the net was loaded with fish. 70 This slowed down our getting to the shore. As we got closer to the shore, one of the disciples cried out, 'It is the Lord!' 71 With that Peter jumped out of the boat and swam to shore. The rest of us arrived in the boat a few minutes later. It was obvious the stranger we had seen from afar was Jesus. 72 We began to pull in the net. We couldn't believe it. There were one hundred fifty-three large fish in the net. We marveled as to why it didn't break. This net was not made to bear such a heavy load."

73 John then told me Jesus invited them all to eat. What he then said, I will never forget. It was, "Mary, can you imagine how we were feeling? We were absolutely overjoyed at seeing Jesus. Now, we were in awe that we were eating a meal he had cooked. **74** He had never cooked a meal during all the years we traveled together. When we traveled with him, there were some of us who took turns caring for meals. Also, often the women traveling with us prepared the meal. Jesus never did. **75** I must confess to you, it was the best fish I had ever eaten. It was absolutely delicious."

76 John also told me, after breakfast, Jesus challenged Peter as to Peter's love for him. He asked Peter three times if he loved him. Peter always responded that he did. Jesus told Peter to feed his sheep and care for them, and especially to care for the lambs. John said it was interesting to him and the other disciples that Peter, who denied the Lord three times, was asked by the Lord three times if he loved him. **77** Jesus also told Peter the time would come when he would be carried by men against his will. This implied he would be crucified. **78** Peter then blurted out, "Well, what about John?" Jesus replied that John's future was none of his business. Even if John were to live until Jesus returned, it should not be a concern of Peter's. **79** The rumor spread John would never die, but John said this was not what Jesus said or meant. Rumors! How quickly they can start, and how ridiculous many of them are. But it seems there is no way you can stop most of them.

80 It was Peter who told me about the day, when Jesus was with some believers, he just started to rise skyward and ultimately disappeared into the clouds. **81** This, of course, was frightening to those who witnessed this strange event. They were shocked and kept staring into the sky. **82** It was then two angels appeared and asked why they just stood there looking up into the heavens. They announced someday Jesus would descend from the sky, as he had ascended. 83 With the words of the angels, his followers were comforted and returned to Jerusalem joyfully worshipping Jesus.

84 I was alone once again. My son was gone somewhere, I knew not where. My visions of earthly glory were once again shattered. My emotions were uncontrollable. I was thrilled that I had seen him alive. I was devastated I would never see him again. 85 Where was he? What was he doing? What should I be doing, and where should I be living? I just couldn't really understand what he had told me in the garden about the future. It just did not make sense to me. 86 Most of my time was spent with the girls in our room. They tried to comfort me, but they didn't understand all these strange happenings any more than I did. I felt my life was again at a hopeless dead end!

Chapter 21

෧෧෬

1 As you know, I didn't immediately return to Nazareth. I sent word to you that the girls and I would be staying in Jerusalem longer than we first thought. I just didn't have the energy to make that long journey, plus I was secretly hoping Jesus would appear to me again. He never did. 2 However, something happened fifty days after his resurrection which completely changed my life. It also miraculously changed the life of each of the disciples, and through the years, the life of hundreds of thousands. 3 Even though we were thrilled to have seen Jesus after his resurrection, all of us were still very discouraged. All of his great teaching and works seemed to have come to an abrupt end. 4 It helped that a number of us to meet together from time to time to console and encourage one another. 5 On the day of Pentecost, there were about one hundred and twenty of us discouraged souls gathered in a large room. Different ones would speak about how they were feeling. Some would relate something Jesus had said to them or done for them. We would spend time praying. 6 Suddenly, and I do mean suddenly, a rushing mighty wind filled the room. We were all scared and frantically looked around to determine which door was open. We thought a terrible storm had developed. There was no open door. Then something even more spectacular happened. We all saw them. 7 Yes, to our

amazement, we saw small 'creatures' which were like tongues of fire. We did not know how they had gotten into the room. These tongues were darting throughout the room. Each one there was personally 'touched' by one of these strange fiery tongue-shaped creatures. We had no idea where they had come from or why they were present.

8 Suddenly, many individuals began to speak at the same time. Amazingly, we couldn't even understand what they were saying. 9 Joses, I can't emphasize enough that we were in a locked room. We were indeed fearful of our lives. Jesus had been killed and we felt it was just a matter of time until some of us would be put in prison, and perhaps even killed. 10 Several minutes after the wind had ceased and the fiery tongues had left, it dawned on us something startling had happened on the inside of each person that was in the room. We each became acutely aware of the fact that all of our fear was gone. I do mean all fear was gone. We felt like we could conquer the world.

11 Peter shouted, "I don't care what happens to me. Open that door! I am going out and preach about Jesus. I am going to the people in the streets just like Jesus did. I am going to explain to people what they have done, and what they ought to be doing." We all cried out, "We are going with you." 12 It didn't take long for all of us to end up in the streets telling about Jesus. Now here is the amazing thing. Even though we were all Jews and spoke Hebrew, we ended up speaking multiple languages which meant everyone we talked to on the streets would understand about Jesus. It didn't matter what nation they were from, they knew what we were saying. This was really astounding.

13 We were also amazed as to how quickly such a large crowd had gathered. People cried out to Peter, "What must we do to be saved?" Many of them were really feeling guilty for how Jesus had been treated. Peter told them to

believe and to be cleansed in their hearts. 14 Hundreds upon hundreds began to believe. In fact, it was reported there were over three thousand who confessed Jesus as Savior and Lord in just one day. 15 It later dawned on us that the teachings of Jesus would soon be all over the world, as those present for Pentecost from many different nations heard the message in their own language. Somehow the Holy Spirit taught them the truths in the teachings of Jesus. It was a miracle how so quickly they understood. They would be taking these truths back home with them. 16 We all definitely realized, and knew, we now had the power Jesus had told us to tarry in Jerusalem and receive. I was so grateful I had remained and had personally experienced this fantastic outpouring of the presence and power of God.

17 Amazing things happened from that day on among the disciples, as well as among many of the common folk. 18 One of the most amazing things was that, after Pentecost, a sizeable number of the Temple priests believed in Jesus. They were truly sorry for what had been done to him. It seemed like a miracle to me how they felt forgiven and that they were very excited about Jesus. I realized John was correct concerning the request of Jesus for the Father to forgive them. I witnessed that they were really being forgiven. 19 John told me Jesus had told the disciples that after he was gone, he would send a Comforter. Well, we now knew he surely kept his word. 20 My deep sorrow was gone. A new joy filled my heart and spirit. Another thing Jesus said about the Holy Spirit was He would teach believers all things. We were amazed how quickly those who confessed Jesus were knowledgeable of what He would have them to believe and do.

21 Jesus had told his disciples that the day would come when they would do the same things he had done, and even greater works. And sure enough, after the day of Pentecost,

miracles began to happen at the hands of the disciples and other believers. **22** Peter and John healed a man at the gate of the Temple, who from his birth, had been an invalid. He had to be carried to the Temple each day to beg for food. But no longer did he have to be carried or beg. He went jumping and leaping into the Temple. He went home rejoicing. **23** Phillip even had people in Samaria accept him and his teachings about Jesus because they saw the miracles he did. **24** Probably the most dramatic day of healing was the day people were healed as Peter walked by them. When his shadow fell upon them, they were healed. It was amazing. **25** In Joppa, Peter even raised a lady from the dead. Yes, the world was dramatically hearing about my Jesus. I must say, we were now beginning to understand the appearance of the fiery tongues. It was God's way of saying that our tongues should be on fire for Jesus. This is what we ended up believing and teaching. **26** By this time, some were saying the followers of Jesus were turning the world upside down. In my heart I felt the ones believing in him, and accepting and living according to his teachings, were turning the world right side up.

27 As you know, I came back to Nazareth about three weeks after Pentecost. I would still be in Nazareth if it were not for John being led by the Spirit to go to Ephesus. **28** I was very grieved when they killed your brother James. He became a devoted follower of Jesus after Pentecost, even though as a young man he felt Jesus was crazy. **29** All of you children and your families have come to believe Jesus to indeed be the Son of God. I am thrilled about this. **30** This thought just came to me, and I will share it before ending this letter. Lazarus lived over thirty years after being raised from the dead. Would you believe the religious leaders at one time were planning to kill Lazarus as well as Jesus? They were never able to carry out their wicked plans for his second death. He never again had a serious illness. 31 In fact, he died one night in his sleep. When he went to bed he was not complaining about any illness. Later in the night, his life on earth ended for the second time. This time, it was painless and quick.

32 After these many years of my pilgrimage of faith, I have come to this conclusion. We are to be givers. Givers of love and mercy. Givers of some of the abundance with which we have been blessed. This especially involves each believer giving to help the poor. 33 One day it really hit me who the ultimate givers are. They are God, the Father, who gave us his Son. God, the Son, who gave to us the Holy Spirit. God, the Holy Spirit, who gave power and spiritual gifts to each believer to be used in the Church. 34 This should instruct and inspire you and me, and all others, to give generously to help others and, in so doing, glorify God.

35 I must tell you what John told me of another thing Jesus said to Thomas. It was after his resurrection and he had been teaching the disciples concerning a number of things. He spent several minutes teaching how his followers should go and share in all nations the message that God loves them and wants to help them. 36 He tried to instill in their minds this was His plan. He made it plain that anyone who loved and served Him should strive to do this. 37 Thomas then asked this question. "Jesus, what if your plan of just ordinary men and women taking your message to the world fails? Then what plan do you have?" 38 Jesus looked at him with a pained expression that conveyed Thomas had evidently missed his whole point. He replied, "Thomas, I have no other plan. I have absolutely no other plan." Joses, I really believe this, and feel his plan must be pursued. 39 I have pondered this statement for hours on end as to how it relates to the many

miraculous things I have witnessed. Many times I have truly seen heaven and earth meet. 40 For instance, I am a very earthly woman and was visited by an angel. In a lowly stable, the Savior of the whole world was born. Very poor humble shepherds heard and saw a multitude of angels from heaven. The wisest of men were instructed by God through the appearance of a promised star. 41 A bleeding man on the cross reconciled men and women to the God of our fathers. A borrowed tomb held, and then released, the Son of God. Unlearned men have been doing unheard of things through the power of the Holy Spirit. 42 The baby born in a lonely stable is now known throughout the whole world. The proclaiming of heavenly truths has been left in the hands of very earthly individuals to impart to others. 43 All of these things are truly amazing to me. In all of them, it is as if heaven and earth are blended together. It is evident that, with God, what we feel is ordinary becomes extraordinary.

Chapter 22

చ°ొ

1 Although I have never been able to explain spiritual encounters, I know they happen. I cannot in any way explain how they happen, but I really believe they do. 2 The good news is heaven has come down, and glory has filled the earth in the lives of those who truly believe. 3 I continue to ponder, how do heaven and earth meet? I do believe they do, but how? I do not know! 4 Isn't it strange there is no one who has an earthly explanation concerning the heavenly things we believe? 5 Whether I have all the answers or not, there is one thing I definitely know: God will accomplish His purposes. For instance, I worried so much about Jesus being born in a stable and how so very few would ever hear about him. But God had it all in His plan and, miraculously, the whole world is hearing about him. 6 As I look back upon it, the humble birth spot certainly reveals that God loves and wants to help even the very lowest of society. He knows what He is doing. We must simply believe Him.

7 In this regard, one of the hardest things for me was how so many could shout loud hosannas and a week later, cry out for Jesus to be crucified. 8 Years later it became clear to me. Thousands shouted the praises of Jesus as he publicly entered Jerusalem. When he had his trial and was condemned to die by crucifixion, only a few even

knew he was in the city. 9 It was definitely not the ordinary Jewish people who had Jesus killed. No, it was a few religious fanatics who organized a mob to cry out for his crucifixion. They had even paid some people to bring false witnesses against Jesus. 10 In reality, he was sincerely cheered by the multitude. They truly loved him. It was really but a few fanatics who actually feared his presence and teachings. They were so obsessed with stopping him from teaching that they even sought his death. He was condemned to death through the actions of a mob. This mob was a much smaller and entirely different group than those who shouted their loud hosannas. 11 The truth is, most of the people present for the Passover never knew Jesus was being crucified until he was seen carrying the cross down the crowded street. Even then it was a much smaller number than had witnessed his triumphant entry into Jerusalem. The news of his being killed had never gotten around like the news of his triumphal entry into the city. 12 Of course, the radical religious leaders didn't want the multitude to know of his being crucified until after it was all over. They would not have dared do it any other way than in as much privacy as possible. Jesus was a threat to their place of power, and greed for money. So they had the Romans kill him. But in the end, God triumphed and brought forth His Son from the grave. 13 So, more than ever, to the best of my ability, I am going to end my days trusting that ultimately all things will be to the glory of the Father who Jesus taught about so much.

14 One of the things I think about the most concerning how Jesus lived and taught was his insights concerning prayer. I was so accustomed to hearing the long prayers of the religious. Frequently they were said on the street corner. Jesus never did that. 15 In fact, he was so different in his prayer life that two of the disciples approached me one day

and asked if I could talk him into teaching them to pray like John the Baptist taught his followers to pray. 16 They said they had talked to Jesus about it, but he seemed to ignore their request. One day I brought the topic up to Jesus. 17 He said, "Mother, prayer should be a talk with the Father. It should not be a time of telling Him all your problems. Nor a time to seek to instruct Him on how you think your prayer should be answered. You shouldn't spend your time in your prayers begging Him to do what you desire. 18 He knows all you have need of, even before you ask Him. So have private conversation with Him. You should really do this in private. You should strive to learn to spend time alone in prayer with the Father, listening to His still small voice. 19 Seek to constantly get more knowledgeable about Him. You won't arrive at that place if you spend time in prayer constantly repeating your problems and fears. 20 He knows all about them. He knows all about you. The need is for you to know more about Him, and His love and power. 21 Prayer should help you accomplish this goal. Your constant chatter will not bring you closer to Him. And Mother, you don't have to worry. My Father will reward you in public for those private quiet times spent with Him. 22 You see, I pray in private. I preach, teach, and heal in public. The religious feel they will be heard for their much praying. They don't understand this is not the path to spiritual power. 23 It is looked upon by the Father as just being a show-off. To the Father, most prayers are an act of disbelief rather than an expression of faith." 24 I must say it seems to me the disciples never did really grasp his teaching on prayer as they should have. I have tried to make his prayer teaching a part of my life, and have found it very helpful.

25 There is so much more I could share, but I don't want to continue to take the time of my friend, as he patiently listens to me and writes what I tell him. 26 Perhaps someday

I will share more of how Jesus was, and still is, a great blessing to me. And not only to me, he is also a blessing to multitudes of others throughout the whole world.

27 There are so many things I have pondered at length through the years. For instance I still can't understand why the religious leaders reacted so negatively toward Jesus. Why didn't they embrace him and his teachings instead of killing him? Surely if his teachings didn't convince them he was from God, then his works of miracles should have. 28 The shepherds really believed he was the Savior of Israel. They believed this concerning a new born baby that was lying in a manger. 29 Now, tell me, does that sound like a place an important person would be born? Of course it is not. Yet they believed. I have often wondered if any of them were aware of Jesus being crucified, and if so, what they then thought of the angel's message to them years before.

30 The religious fanatics just could not believe. Yet, isn't it interesting the Magi were completely convinced he was the King of the Jews? The fact he was a small child, of poor parents, living in a very small house did not destroy their faith in him or lead them to doubt God. 31 They did not hesitate to give this little child the valuable gifts they had brought for a King. It has always been amazing to me how the rich Magi would be so firmly convinced Jesus was the King they were seeking. 32 The religious were familiar with the words of the prophet concerning where Jesus would be born, but were not interested in the fact that the prophet's words had been fulfilled.

33 The fact that he was called King of the Jews by the Roman ruler, Pilate, is a puzzle to me. The religious leaders could in no way accept him as such, but a wicked Gentile at the time of his death wanted to let all Jerusalem know Jesus was King of the Jews. Isn't it strange that the one you

would least expect to do so would proclaim him King of the Jews?

34 Just take a few moments and think about it. Neither the shepherds, Magi, nor Pilate witnessed any of the miracles of Jesus, but they believed he was special. On the other hand, many of the religious witnessed many of his miracles. Some even witnessed Lazarus being raised from the dead. Regardless of these miracles, they ended up being among those who wanted to kill him.

35 Down through the years I have noticed how some readily believe in Jesus. However, the large majority of individuals are simply not convinced. They desire to go their own way instead of sincerely seeking to serve God by serving others. 36 I still remember the time Jesus and I were talking about the fact that some truly believed, but many did not. I asked him why some really believe and follow him. He said, "Mother, you must realize they have not chosen me, but I have chosen them. I chose them to fulfill my Father's will for them." 37 His answer is one I have yet to fully understand. I want to assure you I still believe in him, and his teachings, regardless of what others do. By the way, speaking of believing in spite of circumstances reminds me of the words of the prophet. 38 Bocheru sometimes reads some of the ancient scriptures to me and his wife. We love to have him do this. 39 One of the portions I remember is the statement of faith of the prophet, Habakkuk. *"Although the fig tree shall not blossom, neither shall fruit be in the vines, the labor of the olive shall fail, and the fields shall yield no meat; the flock shall be cut off from the fold, and there shall be no herd in the stalls. Yet I will rejoice in the Lord, I will joy in the God of my salvation."* This is the faith I have and will continue to have.

40 I almost forgot to include this important truth. I well remember how his blood covered his body. Also, how it gushed forth when the soldier's spear pierced his side. I was overwhelmed with anguish as I witnessed these cruel acts. 41 I now realize Jesus permitted his blood to be shed to reconcile the whole world to the Father. Thus, his death on the cross, as horrible as it was, served a very worthy purpose. 42 The shedding of his blood brought life for those who believe. It was in this way that he became the one to reconcile the world with the Father.

43 John told me that the reason he talks to individuals about Jesus is because we are to be reconcilers. We must seek to persuade individuals to be reconciled to the Father through Jesus. 44 It is a simple message, but one that I did not grasp during the time Jesus lived with us. I am so grateful I understand it now. My understanding has become so much greater since the coming of the Holy Spirit. 45 I have also been helped a lot through the many hours John and I have spent talking about Jesus and his wonderful teachings.

46 You have had enough of my rambling. Many weeks have passed since I started this letter to you. I didn't think this letter would be this long or take so many weeks to complete. 47 Parts of it have been very emotional moments for me. I have re-lived some of my very difficult times. I may have repeated myself at times. However, I pray that it will help you better understand your brother, Jesus. 48 Please share my letter with other members of the family, and also with as many of your friends as possible. It may be of interest and a very likely a help to them.

49 I am getting more anxious each passing day to be with your father, and with my precious Jesus. The anticipated joy of seeing them and spending eternity with them sustains me in the lonely hours of the night, and the uncertainties of the days.

50 May the blessings of the God of our fathers and the precious presence of your brother Jesus, be with you and also be with your family. 51 I am sure John would want me to extend his greetings to you. I constantly pray he will soon be permitted to return from exile. I miss him so much. He has been so good to me through so many of the difficult times I have had to face. He has comforted me in my fears and strengthened me when my faith has faltered.

52 How I yearn to see you and my other children, and all of my grandchildren. Please do come to Ephesus soon. I yearn for your visit. 53 I want you to meet my friend, Bocheru. He has been so faithful and patient in writing this letter for me and I know he wrote it well despite some of my ramblings. Certainly it has not been easy, but he and his wife have been true and compassionate friends. May God's blessings ever be with them and their children, for all the kindness extended to me.

54 This letter has ended up much longer than I had ever dreamed, however there is so much to tell. Even now I think of things I should have included, but I can't impose on Bocheru's time any longer.

55 Before I close, I must ask you to do what you can to have my letter read in the churches in your area. I hear this has happened to some of the Apostle Paul's letters, and the reading of them has been a powerful tool in gaining and encouraging believers. I miss you so much.

56 Your loving mother, *Mary*.

Modern Update

ॐ

An update for our day seems appropriate. Mary's fears of Jesus not being known to the world turned out to be unjustified. His teachings have spread throughout the entire world and beyond. On July 20, 1969, Buzz Aldrin privately observed Holy Communion on the moon. Yes, billions of individuals all over the world have acknowledged Jesus as their Savior and Lord since he was born in that stinking stable.

The Bible, with the New Testament focused on Jesus, is the bestselling book of all time. Millions and millions of copies of all or parts of it have been translated, printed and distributed in every nation of the world. Further, even though declining in western culture, Christianity is the fastest growing religion in the world today. It is especially spreading rapidly in developing nations.

It certainly has been proven time and again that ordinary unlearned individuals can do extraordinary things when empowered by God. It is a strange twist of history that most of the highly educated in the days of Jesus have long since been forgotten. The names of the uneducated twelve are known to billions, and will be known until the end of time.

Mary's premonition John would write certainly came true. He is credited with writing five of the twenty-seven books of the New Testament. They are the Gospel of John, First, Second, Third John, and the book of Revelation. We also have writings credited to two others of the original twelve apostles. They are The Gospel of Matthew, and First and Second Peter.

The ordinary truly becomes the extraordinary when Mary, the humble unknown Jewish teenager, has become the most famous mother in the entire world.

May you realize *The Gospel According to Mary, Mother of Jesus* is an excellent modern way for you to spread the Good News of the old, old story. May you encourage your family members, friends, and acquaintances to read *The Gospel According to Mary, Mother of Jesus*. You may also purchase copies as a gift for those close to you, as well as distribute in your church, especially to the youth. If you are a business owner, you can spread the Christian message in a modern way by providing a copy of *The Gospel According to Mary, Mother of Jesus* for your employees, and have them for sale at your establishment.

Discussion Questions

❧❧

To enhance group discussion and individual meditation.

Chapter 1

1. *What is your reaction to a novel that has Mary writing about the life of Jesus?*

2. *What do you believe may be the reasons ten of the twelve disciples were killed?*

3. *Do you believe angels appear to individuals today? Explain.*

Chapter 2

1. *What is your reaction to the ideas presented throughout the book concerning the gifts of the Magi?*

2. *Do you feel Jesus deliberately broke with tradition? Explain.*

3. *Do you feel the Christian life is different than the life of society as a whole? Explain.*

Notes: _____

_____

_____

_____

Chapter 3

1. *What is your appraisal of Mary's response to the rumor that Jesus was her only child? Explain.*

2. *Do you feel the siblings of Jesus were justified in thinking he was crazy? Explain.*

3. *Do you feel most people today believe Jesus actually did miracles? Explain.*

Chapter 4

1. *Do you feel the suggested obstacles Mary faced being a pregnant virgin could have really happened to her? Explain.*

2. *Do you feel Joseph's reactions are natural ones? Explain.*

3. *Have you ever thought of the fact Mary could have been stoned to death? Explain.*

4. *Have you, or anyone you know, ever seen an angel? If yes, give details.*

Chapter 5

1. *Have you ever come in contact with a person where you felt a strong spiritual presence surrounding them? Explain.*

2. *What is the difference between being religious and being spiritual?*

3. *Is church life as we know it today religious or spiritual? Explain.*

Notes: _____

_____

_____

_____

Chapter 6

1. Do you think Mary was justified in thinking Jesus should be widely known from the time he was born? Explain.

2. Were you aware of the fact the stable where Jesus was born was a cave? Explain.

3. Was Mary justified in trying to make sure Jesus was born in a place where the world would hear about him? Explain.

Chapter 7

1. Why do you feel God had His angels announce the birth of His Son to lowly shepherds?

2. Do you feel many people are aware of the real presence of God today? Explain.

3. Do you feel God still uses ordinary people to do extraordinary things? Explain.

Chapter 8

1. Why do you feel the religious leaders missed the significance of Jesus, while Simeon and Anna were aware of it?

2. Did you know that the wise men came sometime after Jesus was born, and that Mary and Joseph were living in a house at that time? Explain.

3. Do you feel there are some today as power oriented as Herod was? Explain.

Notes: _____

_____

_____

_____

_____

_____

Chapter 9

1. *Why do you feel the religious leaders showed so little interest concerning the birth of Jesus?*

2. *Has there ever been what seemed an insignificant thing happen in your life which later, you realized it was really very important? Explain.*

3. *Do you feel there are people today who would like to eliminate all spiritual emphasis in our nation? Explain.*

Chapter 10

1. *Do you feel some people seem to be more attune to God speaking to them through their dreams? Explain.*

2. *What ways do you feel God uses to speak to individuals today?*

3. *Is there as much cruelty in the world today, as in the days of Herod? Explain.*

Chapter 11

1. *Do you feel that some children are more spiritually sensitive than most children? Explain.*

2. *Have you ever known any child that you felt was destined for some leadership area, such as the religious leaders perceived of Jesus? Explain.*

3. *How important is the spiritual teaching and example of parents to their children?*

Notes: _____

_____

_____

_____

_____

_____

Chapter 12

1. *Why do you feel Mary felt Jesus could do something to solve the problem of the lack of wine at the wedding feast?*

2. *Are people today inclined to look upon things as the answer instead of God, as the host looked to the jars as the reason for the water turning to wine? Explain.*

3. *Do you feel, if you really believed, you could see miracles in your life? Why or why not?*

Chapter 13

1. *Why do you feel so many people went to hear John the Baptist preach?*

2. *Jesus was tested for forty days and nights while alone in the desert. Do you feel a person is more likely to sense and know the presence and power of God when away from the hustle and struggles of everyday life? Explain.*

3. *Has any incident in your life changed your spiritual outlook? Explain.*

Chapter 14

1. *Why do you feel Jesus chose unlearned and out-of-the-religious-circle disciples?*

2. *What is the significance of the Holy Spirit in the life of a believer today?*

3. *What is your reaction to the teaching that you should repent from believing God doesn't love you?*

Notes: _____

_____

_____

_____

Chapter 15

1. *What is your reaction to the emphasis that you should repent from believing God doesn't want to help you?*

2. *How do you feel about the fact Jesus reduced all the myriad of laws and regulations to: a. Love God; and, b. Love others?*

3. *What is your reaction to the teaching that is important to repent from believing religion can save you?*

Chapter 16

1. *How did you react to the author's details surrounding Lazarus being raised from the dead?*

2. *Do you think Mary really thought often about Jesus becoming the King of the Jews? Explain.*

3. *What do you feel happens to a person after they die?*

Chapter 17

1. *How sincere do you feel the multitude was that welcomed Jesus the day of his triumphal entry into Jerusalem?*

2. *Do you feel a few people acting as a mob can do a great deal of damage? Explain.*

3. *Do you feel that a lot of government action today is done in secret, and would never happen if the general public knew what was going on?*

Notes: _____

_____

_____

_____

_____

_____

Chapter 18

1. *Are the actions of Pilate similar to what most of us would do when facing a difficult decision that could affect our job or status in society?*

2. *Why do you think Pilate put the sign* **"Jesus of Nazareth, King of the Jews"** *on the cross?*

3. *What was your reaction to the expressed feelings of Mary as she witnessed the crucifixion?*

Chapter 19

1. *What is your reaction to Mary crying out for an angel to come and rescue Jesus?*

2. *What did Jesus mean when he said, "It is finished!"*

3. *What message does Jesus being born in a stable and buried in a borrowed tomb have for believers today?*

Chapter 20

1. *Why did Jesus say, "No Mary, God's Son," when she cried out to him "My dear son?"*

2. *Do you feel "doubting Thomas" is typical of most of us? Explain.*

3. *What did Jesus mean when he told Peter to care for my sheep and my lambs?*

Notes: _____

_____

_____

_____

_____

_____

_____

Chapter 21

1. Can the power of the Holy Spirit be received today as on the day of Pentecost? Explain.

2. What is your reaction to Mary saying she is convinced we are to be givers, because God the Father gave His Son, God the Son gave the Holy Spirit, and the Holy Spirit gave power and spiritual gifts to the Church?

3. What is your reaction to the fact Jesus told Thomas he had no other plan than believers taking his message to the world?

Chapter 22

1. Do you agree with Mary's insight that the crowd welcoming Jesus into the city was an entirely different group of people than those who cried "Crucify him!"? Explain.

2. In what ways in her Gospel do you feel Mary tells the Good News of the Gospel as revealed by Jesus?

3. How has the reading of The Gospel According to Mary, Mother of Jesus *affected you?*

Notes: _____

_____

_____

_____

_____

_____

_____

_____

_____

_____

Biblical Index

❧

In this Biblical Index, the verse is listed when Mary writes concerning a topic that appears in the Bible. To the right of this verse is listed the Biblical reference. Throughout the book, the number of the verse with a Bible reference is in bold type.

For greater understanding, you may desire to read some verses prior to, and following, the listed Bible reference. The *King James Version* is the one quoted and referred to in this book.

Chapter 1

Chapter2

Chapter 3

Chapter 7

Chapter 8

Chapter 9

Chapter 10

Chapter 14

Chapter 15

Chapter 16

Chapter 17

88 .... John 18:11

90 .... John 18:10

96 .... Luke 23:51

100 .... Acts 10:38

102 .... Matthew 20:17; Mark 10:33, 34;
Luke 18:31-34

Chapter 18

1. .... Matthew 26:59, 60

2 .... Matthew 27:2

3 .... Luke 23:7

4 .... John 19:15

6 .... Matthew 27:19

8 .... Luke 23:4

11 .... John 18:39, 40

12 .... John 19:15

13 .... Matthew 27:24

14 .... Matthew 27:25

16 .... Matthew 27:28

17 .... Matthew 27:29

24 .... Matthew 27:32

43 .... Matthew 27:37

Chapter 19

Chapter 20

Chapter 21

Chapter 22

Scripture Cross-References

ৰ্ু৵৽

The following are the scriptures concerning topics discussed by Mary in her letter to Joses. They are listed in biblical sequence. Beside each scripture reference is the location where the topic is coincided in *The Gospel According to Mary, Mother of Jesus*.

Genesis .... **Mary**
15:6................................14:22

Numbers .... **Mary**
24:17................................8:34

Judges .... **Mary**
13:5................................10:34

Isaiah .... **Mary**
7:14................................4:69

Jeremiah .... **Mary**
31:15..............................10:22
31:33..............................2:40

Daniel .... **Mary**
3:21-27...........................1:61

Hosea .... **Mary**
11:1................................10:22

26:75 .... 17:53
27:2 .... 18:2
27:5 .... 17:58
27:19 .... 18:6
27:24 .... 18:13
27:25 .... 18:14
27:28 .... 18:16
27:29 .... 18:17
27:32 .... 18:24
27:37 .... 18:43
27:45 .... 19:23
27:46 .... 19:27
27:51 .... 19:40
27:52-54 .... 19:42
27:54 .... 19:25
27:57 .... 19:48
27:62-66 .... 20:5
27:62-66 .... 20:6
28:19 .... 21:35

Mark .... Mary
3:14, 15 .... 15:6
3:35 .... 3:10
6:2 .... 3:41
6:3 .... 3:38
6:5 .... 3:42
6:7 .... 15:6
6:13 .... 15:6
7:26 .... 15:5
8:23 .... 2:34
9:23 .... 14:18
10:33, 34 .... 17:102
14:26 .... 17:61
15:34 .... 19:27
16:6 .... 2:32
16:7 .... 17:57

Luke .... Mary

4:14................................14:17
4:18................................14:30
4:30................................3:46
7:9..................................15:4
9:1,2...............................15:6
10:17..............................15:7
14:12-14 ....14:41
18:31-34 ....17:102
19:1-8 ....14:43
19:41..............................17:13
22:36-38 ....17:72
23:4................................18:8
23:7................................18:3
23:34..............................19:13
23:39..............................19:16
23:42..............................19:18
23:43..............................19:20
23:46..............................19:32
23:51..............................17:96
24:2................................20:12
24:13..............................20:58
24:51..............................2:32
24:51..............................20:80

John .... Mary
1:36................................13:8
2:1..................................12:14
2:7..................................12:18
2:10................................12:24
2:11................................12:26
3:1, 2..............................19:50
3:7..................................19:51
3:16................................14:27
3:18................................14:19
4:13, 14..........................2:2
5:9..................................2:35
6:10, 11..........................15:8

Other Books by Donald W. Bartow

Bartow's Healing Handbook

A must book for every home! Blends prayer and healing in one book, offers solid Biblical teaching, is a good guide for study, and contains the 30-Day Prayer Pilgrimage.

Yes, Virginia, There Is A God Who Heals Today

Join Virginia as she exchanges e-mails with Pastor Bartow, asking questions and getting answers to important topics. Delightful and compelling reading! It presents scriptural and practical reasons for spiritual healing, helping the poor, repentance, the power of prayer, and being born again.

Praying His Promises

A detailed consideration of the prayer lifestyle of Jesus as revealed in the Gospels. Also, specific guidance is given as to how to pray the Scriptures. The model prayers deal with the everyday areas of concern, such as fear, worry, illness, finances, loneliness, depression, praise, blessing, God's presence, and more.

The Challenge to Believe

This scripturally sound and very practical book presents insights in how to be a winner with God, who loves us and wants to help us.

Share the Blessings of

The Gospel According to Mary, Mother of Jesus

You may obtain additional copies of *The Gospel According to Mary, Mother of Jesus* from: The author, www.wholenesspublications.com, Amazon.com, and your local bookstore.

It is available in Hardcover, E-Book, Audio Book and Large Print formats.

About the Author

Throughout his many years in the ministry, Pastor Donald W. Bartow has authored over 25 books and traveled nationally for guest appearances on TV, radio, and conferences. His books have covered a wide array of Biblical topics expounding on principles and truths which apply to both individuals and churches. His extensive ministry has endeavored to help people live significantly with and for God. Expanding his vision to help others, he launched and directs *The Total Living Center*, an outreach ministry in Canton, Ohio

In his latest book, *The Gospel According to Mary, Mother of Jesus*, the reader will grasp the reality that ordinary people can experience and do very extraordinary things. In this insightful work, one gripping truth prevails — God will accomplish His purposes! Teen-ager, devoted Bible reader, or one who never reads the Bible, you will love Mary's personal, informative and easy to read Gospel.

Contact Pastor Don Bartow

Pastor Bartow would love to receive your comments concerning *The Gospel According to Mary, Mother of Jesus*. Also, please share with him ways in which you are spreading the Good News of the old, old story through your sharing of *The Gospel According to Mary, Mother of Jesus*. You may contact him in one of the following ways:

Mail: 2221 Ninth Street, SW

P.O. Box 36057

Canton, Ohio 44735

E-Mail: DonBartow@wholenesspublications.com

Web Site: www.wholenesspublications.com

Facebook: https://www.facebook.com/gospelaccordingtomary

Phone: (330) 437-1635

Toll Free: (888) 799-6923